HOME TO BINDARRA CREEK

A Bindarra Creek Romance

JUANITA KEES

HOME TO BINDARRA CREEK

A BINDARRA CREEK ROMANCE BY

JUANITA KEES

Juanita Kees

CONTENTS

EXCERPT - PROMISE ME FOREVER

Home to Bindarra Creek.

Published by Juanita Kees

978-0-6484995-1-0 Ebook
978-0-6484995-0-3 Paperback
978-0-6484995-2-7 Large Print
Cover Design © Paradox Book Cover and Formatting
Edited by Belinda Holmes

ACKNOWLEDGEMENTS

This book would never have been written were it not for the fabulous ladies from the Hunter Romance Writers who so kindly invited this West Aussie to join them in this venture. What a pleasure it's been to work with such a talented and organized group of authors. We created a town we all wanted to live in. Thank you.

To my wonderful critique partners: Kerrie Paterson, SE Gilchrist, Jennie Jones, Lily Malone, Claire Boston, Nora James, Susanna Rogers, Anna Jacobs and Teena Raffa-Mulligan – your input is magic. You've helped me craft a book with heart.

My beta reader, Anne O'Dell, who gives me such wonderfully honest feedback – you're a treasure.

Not to be forgotten, my editor Belinda Holmes – you make me smile with your wonderfully uplifting comments and suggestions.

DEDICATION

This book is for lovers of small town romance world-wide, but if I were to dedicate this story to any one person in particular, it would be to Len Klumpp, who is a tireless supporter of Australian Rural Romance authors.

Len, you rock!

A BINDARRA CREEK ROMANCE

Drama, intrigue, suspense, adventure and honest, country goodness – welcome to Bindarra Creek where life and love in a small country town has never been more challenging.

*D*an Molyneaux eased his V8 sedan around the bend and into the straight with the effortlessness of an experienced driver who enjoyed the power in his hands and the roar of the engine under the hood. Out here in the country with no traffic on the road for miles, he could push it to the speed limit and blow the cobwebs from the pistons. Just the way he liked it. If only it was as easy to erase the guilt from his heart.

He accelerated up the hill to the rise ahead, preparing for the drop that would lie beyond. His heart pumped hard with adrenaline in anticipation of the downward slope to come. The g-force would drag at his abs and suck the breath from his lungs on a *Yes!*

For the first time in months, he was free. Unchained from a desk job that had destroyed his faith in humanity and a million-dollar view that was no compensation for his mistakes.

The downhill came and didn't disappoint, but as the road stretched out in front of him and momentum carried him towards the next bend, a kangaroo burst from the bush onto the road. He braked—hard and fast—the red alert flashing on his screen display, warning him of the impending impact. He knew if he swerved to avoid the animal, he'd roll the car or hit a tree or worse, kill himself. The rear end fishtailed and as he struggled to control the skid, the front end collided with the roo and rolled it onto the hood. The impact of its head against the glass sent cracks running across the windscreen.

"Fuck!"

He steered into the curve of the road as he stepped harder on the brakes, the stench of burning rubber in his nostrils, and felt the drag of the automatic braking system as it slowed the travel. The car rolled to a stop in the ditch and the cabin filled with the burning smell of death.

Dan's hands shook on the wheel. His heart pumped hard in his chest, and even though he knew there was nothing he could have done to avoid hitting the roo, guilt rushed at him. More blood on his hands.

"Damn it!"

For a moment he sat gathering his wits, calming his pulse, mentally calculating his speed at point of impact. Even though he hadn't been over the speed limit, the emergency braking system would only have shaved off a quarter of the speed before the car hit. Eighty kilometres per hour. If the roo was alive, it would be pretty beat up. Not the animal's lucky day and certainly not his either.

His heart still pounding, he stared at the roo lying prone on the hood, its snout only inches from his own nose. Only centimetres and a wrecked sheet of glass had stood between him and death or at the very least, serious injury.

Once again, he stared death in the face. The glassy eyes of the roo staring back at him brought back visions of another death where the sightless eyes were human.

He pushed open the car door, the metallic squawk from the hinges warning him of the damage to expect. With a wary eye on the roo, he stepped out onto the bitumen where thick tracks of rubber layered the road, evidence of his close shave. Keeping his distance, he examined the wreck. Spidery veins spread around the hole in the windscreen, the only thing maintaining the concave shape and stopping it from collapsing was the shatterproof film. The hood wore the indent of the kangaroo's body pressed into the metal, and the front end formed a perfect vee. Dan wasn't sure who was worse off, the car or the kangaroo. The car could be fixed but he thought it might be too late for the roo.

He checked his phone. Thank God he had a signal. It meant he wasn't in the middle of nowhere, miles away from civilisation. Who to call? Mum first, because she was expecting him. She'd be worried if he didn't show up on time. Plus, after almost twelve months in the backwater town of Bindarra Creek, she'd know who to call for a tow. Next, he'd call the insurance company. He pressed out his mother's number and waited for her to answer.

"Dan! Where are you?"

"Hey, Mum. Don't panic, I'm okay. I had a little accident." He raked a still shaky hand through his hair. "I hit a roo."

The familiar sound of her voice eased over the shock, reminding him of his childhood—when it was just the two of them, when she'd encouraged him to spread his wings and been there to patch up his

4

wounds when he'd fallen. Warmth flooded his heart, filling a little of the void that plagued him. He should have made an effort to see her before now.

He clenched his jaw. There'd been nothing stopping him from making the trip sooner except he'd been too busy ruining people's lives with investments doomed to fail. Perhaps that's why he hadn't thought twice about investing in a rundown pub in a nowhere town—penance for his sins. If he failed, he'd be kissing a couple of hundred thousand of his invested dollars goodbye. He hoped to God that hitting the roo wasn't another sign of Karma having a field day with his life.

"Oh Dan, honey. Are you okay? Where?"

Dan looked around for a signpost, anything that might give him a clue. "About forty k's from Bindarra Creek."

"Oh, honey! Not a good way to start your new life, is it?"

He scratched his head then pressed his fingertips to his gritty eyes. "No, it isn't." God, he must be close to burnout if his eyes stung more for the dead kangaroo than they did for his equally dead V8.

"Hang in there, Dan. I'll give our local mechanic a call to come down and tow you in."

"I can call it in, Mum. Give me his number. I'll

have to give him my insurance details anyway." He lifted his head at the sound of an engine gearing down and the swish of tyres on gravel. The yellow rotating lights flashed on the light bar of the white four-wheel drive ute, illuminating the signwriting on the hood—Bindarra Creek National Park Ranger. "Looks like help in some form has arrived. The ranger just pulled up."

His mum chuckled. "That'll be Alice. She'll take care of you and the roo. Leave the rest to me. It's not like you're going to do a runner on old Fred. He can get all the nitty-gritty details from you later. Besides, you're going to have your hands full in a minute, filling out Alice's environmental accident reports."

"Great! And here I was thinking I was done with paperwork. Thanks, Mum," he said and pressed the end call button. *Alice?* The name echoed in his head, but the shock of the accident had clouded his mind and he pushed aside the niggling feeling he should know the name.

Hand on the buckled roof frame of his car, Dan watched as the ranger got out of the ute and walked toward him, the butt of her rifle balanced against her shoulder, the barrel pointed to the ground. The thunderous expression on her face and the grim, tight line of her lips had him praying the rifle was meant for the roo and not for him. She stopped a few feet in front of him and eyed the damage to the car. Without a word, she brushed past him and headed for the kangaroo. Rifle ready, she aimed for the head.

Dan's heart lurched in his throat. "You're going to shoot it?"

She threw him a black look over her shoulder. "It's the quickest way to put her out of her misery. It's what we have to do when motorists wipe them out."

The way she said *motorist* twisted his gut. The disdain, the hatred, the hurt. No, the feisty ranger wasn't enjoying this any more than he was. "I'm sorry. It was just there. I could never have stopped in time without hitting a tree and killing myself. It's dead."

Dan caught a look at her paling features as she turned away and aimed again. Her words were unsteady when she spoke. "Roos are clever at playing dead. It's their safety mechanism. No matter how bad their injuries are they run on adrenalin—just like humans. If their legs are broken, they'll still get up, kick the shit out of you and run away, only to die from shock and injuries somewhere in the bush."

She approached the roo cautiously, rifle ready. The roo lifted its head, brown eyes round and wide.

It struggled to lift the weight of its body, rolled off the hood, shuddered and fell onto the road. Dan swallowed the grim taste of bile in his throat and looked away as the shot rang through the air, sending parrots squawking into the air from the trees.

"Make yourself useful, City Boy. There's a blue tarp in the back of the ute. Bring it and help me drag her onto it." She threw the command at him without even looking back as she explored the body of the roo. "And while you're there, bring me the little blue sleeping bag. She has a joey."

Shock, anger, regret—the emotions warred inside him as he stood frozen to the spot. How could he have thought a tree change would make a difference? What was he thinking? Even out here in the middle of nowhere he was ruining lives, destroying families. The black pull of anxiety tugged at the far reaches of his mind.

He *could* quit now and go back to his corner office with the view of the Sydney Harbour Bridge and the comfort zone of short office hours and long lunches. But then he'd never know if he *could* cut it in the country or not, and he'd never been one to back down from a challenge. His gaze dropped to his hands where traces of blood from the doorframe had marked his skin—another death on his conscience, another growing bloodstain on the ground to confront him in his nightmares.

He heard the crunch of Alice's boots on the gravel and felt the whoosh of air as she walked past him to the ute. She returned moments later with a pouch under her arm and a small bottle of water and roll of toilet paper in her hands.

"Here," she said, thrusting the bottle and toilet paper under his nose. "Clean up and get the tarp."

Merciless, he thought. Not that he didn't deserve the ranger's anger. He should have known better, expected something like this to happen. He'd read the sad statistics on road kill. Too late now—there was no going back. He wiped the blood from his hands with the water and toilet paper, then turned in time to see Alice heading towards him with the blue pouch in her arms. All he saw as she brushed past him was a tiny furry head, all eyes, ears and snout, peering out from the gap in the pouch.

He followed her to the ute, watching as she laid the pouch on the front seat against the backrest and secured it with the seatbelt. She reeked of roo poo and the coppery stench of blood and gunpowder. His stomach rolled again and he swallowed hard against the rising memory of another time when the smell of death had haunted his senses. Perspiration built on his forehead as he fought to keep the rising bile down.

Alice eyed him wryly. "If you throw up, I'll make you walk the forty kilometres into town," she growled. "You should get there by midnight."

Dan stepped back, took a breath and walked around the back of the ute to grab the tarp. He found himself smiling grimly. Roo poo and all, she was a fresh change from the city girls. He couldn't imagine any of them doing what Alice had. Sure, she was angry and bad-tempered right now—she had the right to be—but under that khaki shirt, those jeans and boots was a pretty neat package. There was definitely something about her, an earthiness that made her real.

He wiped his palms on the backside of his jeans and pulled the tarp over the side of the ute, slinging it over his shoulder. A shaft of pain speared through his chest. Seatbelt burn for his sins, and no doubt tomorrow his muscles would be screaming from the force of impact.

On the way back to the kangaroo, he cast a sad look at his car. Only two thousand k's on the clock and it was probably a write-off. He'd made a typical city boy error. He should have bought something sturdier, something more suited to the country, like Alice's four-wheel drive.

Alice sat crouched at the kangaroo's side. Silently, he spread the tarp out on the ground and waited for instruction. It was then he noticed the two white crosses at the foot of the giant eucalypt. *RIP Lochie. RIP Pete.* A shiver ran through him. If he'd swerved to avoid the animal, his name could have been on a cross there too.

"Take the tail, Slick. I'll get the light bit."

He looked down to see Alice peering up at him, her arms under the kangaroo's shoulders, ready to shift it onto the tarp. Casting off his morbid thought, he moved to lift the tail. "You're going to pick up that roo."

"That's what I said."

"That thing must weigh a ton."

"It's a female. She's only about forty kilos. What? You think I can't do it?"

"I never said that."

"Then put your back into it before we become a statistic ourselves. On the count of three," said Alice. "One, two, three!"

They placed the roo onto the tarp, carried it to the ute and laid it out on the tray. Alice leapt up into the back and wrapped the carcass firmly in the tarp, tying it up with rope. Jumping back down, she slapped the tailgate shut and snapped the locks into place. Her phone rang and she whipped it out of the top pocket of her shirt.

"Hey, Fred," she greeted warmly. "Yeah, I'm okay. Sure, of course. I'll tell him. What?" The change in her tone—from warm to freezing in seconds—had Dan's head snapping up. She looked at him with a frown and then looked away again, listening to what her caller had to say. "Just my luck. I'll drop him off at Maureen's. Cheers, mate."

Dan waited as she hung up and opened the driver's door of the ute. She tossed the phone on the seat and unbuckled the bundled joey.

"Here, you'll have to hold the joey on the drive back into town. Fred will be down later to tow in your car." The chill in her tone froze any response he might make. "Get in. I'll give you a lift to your mum's."

Wordlessly, he took the joey and hoisted himself into the passenger seat of the ute. As she slid behind the wheel, he wondered what it was that had swung her mood from angry to freeze-out.

Alice breathed and tried not to take in the scent of expensive male cologne filling the cab, or the less inviting pong of roo poo. The latter she was used to, the former brought back too many painful memories.

When she'd spotted the car and roo on her routine patrol to check for road kill, she almost hadn't stopped, was tempted to keep driving past that goddamn tree and ring the accident in to triple zero instead. Why? Why had Dan Molyneaux chosen that spot to run into trouble?

It had taken every ounce of strength she had to pull over at the very same place she'd lost her husband and child. The little white crosses, the scarred base of the tree, even the ditch Dan had ended up in—all of them stark reminders of the crash. If he'd swerved, the tree would have claimed another life, and she couldn't have stopped for that. No way in hell.

Her hands shook on the steering wheel and she gripped it tighter, knuckles white against the black leather. Grandad Charlie would have her head if he found out how rude she'd been to Dan. He'd tell her it wasn't the man's fault and things happen for a reason. A sign, he'd call it, a sign it was time to move on.

She snuck a look at the man beside her. Tall with

dark brown hair, he was good looking enough to be a model for *Tractor Weekly*, except he was a city boy. She caught the look that softened his features as he gazed down at the joey cuddled to his chest in big strong arms. She watched his long fingers gently stroke the rough fur of its ears then run down the line on its snout. Her stomach clenched with awareness at the tenderness in his touch. No way would she let herself like him for that show of caring. She wanted to hate the man who'd bought the Riverside Pub.

"What happens to the joey now?" he asked, breaking into her thoughts.

"I get him checked out at the vet." She'd never intended to sell the pub, it had been in her family for as long as the town had existed, but with the rejuvenation of Bindarra Creek town, Charlie had convinced her it was time to let go of the past.

"And then?"

She sighed, annoyed at having to make conversation with him. It should have been easy. Sign the pub over, hand him the key and walk away without ever having to step inside the place again. She hadn't opened the door in eight years and she wasn't about to do so now.

"We find him a carer until he's old enough to feed himself, teach him how to be a kangaroo and then set him free where we found him." Oh God, and that meant going back to the tree again—another damn good reason to dislike the man sitting next to her.

Bindarra Creek was a small town, but not so small that she'd run into him every five minutes. She kept herself busy enough to avoid the town events and social gatherings, so avoiding him should be just as easy. Driving past Riverside every day and seeing the doors open for business again would be like a stake to her heart because as surely as Dan Molyneaux had killed that kangaroo, the Riverside Pub had killed her husband and child.

Out the corner of her eye, she glimpsed Dan running a hand through his GQ-styled hair. Everything about him screamed success. So what was an up-and-coming exec doing in their little backwater town? Suspicion reared its ugly head. Her own reservations aside, with developers flooding into town and scammers taking advantage of it, she held more than a little resentment towards the council's idea of rejuvenation. But as Charlie had so wisely said, it was the only way to stop Bindarra Creek becoming another ghost town on the map. Not that it was much more than that at the moment.

As the town came into view, Dan spoke. "Look,

I'm really sorry about the kangaroo. If I could have stopped in time, I would have. I feel really shit. I've never killed so much as a cockroach in my life."

Alice threw him a doubtful look before slowing down to the forty-kilometre per hour speed limit at the entry to Main Street.

He sighed and tried again. "You obviously already know who I am because you're taking me to Mum's, but I'll introduce myself anyway. I'm Dan Molyneaux. I bought the Riverside Pub."

And by God, he sounded so friggin' chuffed with himself—like a kid with a new toy at Christmas. Her grip tightened on the wheel again and she bit back a sharp retort. Anger—irrational and totally uncalled for—rose hot and fast through her blood. If she'd known what an emotional rollercoaster it would be making the decision to sell, she would have dug her feet in deeper and said no. She took a deep breath and let it out slowly. "I know. I'm the one who sold it to you."

"God bless Karma for introducing us so badly," he mocked. "I am pleased to meet you, Alice. I wish it was under better circumstances." He rubbed the sleeping joey's ears. "I'm sorry I didn't recognise your name before."

She ignored him as she turned into the driveway

of the veterinary clinic. A touch of guilt trickled through her. He wasn't to know the whole story. No-one had spoken of the tragic events leading to the accident almost eight years ago, nor had anyone murmured a word when she'd shut the doors and boarded up the windows of the two-storey building overlooking the Akuna River. Charlie had silently helped her move from the upstairs accommodation and into the house at the wildlife sanctuary across Gillies Bridge, where the view of the pub was obscured by the trees.

"Yeah, me too," she said, pulling to a stop in front of the clinic. "I'll drop the joey off first." Getting out of the ute, she walked around and opened his door, holding her arms out for the joey.

Dan went to unclip his seatbelt. "I'll come with you. Make sure he's okay."

"This isn't an episode of *Skippy*, Mr Molyneaux. I take him inside, the vet checks him out and keeps him overnight. This is where your responsibility ends. The rest is up to me."

God, she hated sounding so damn angry. Raw pain slashed at her heart. Why did the man responsible for forcing her out of her comfort zone have to be so friggin' nice when all she could be in return was bitchy? Right now, all she wanted was to curl up in the corner and cry as old wounds reopened and bled inside her.

Until today the sale had been nothing more than a piece of paper, but now the new owner was here in the flesh, reality confronted her with the speed of a freight train.

Dan frowned down at her, but handed over the joey in silence. She took it and cradled it close to her chest, tears choking her throat. Turning away so he wouldn't see them fill her eyes, she hurried toward the clinic.

Dan let out a breath as he watched Alice walk away. Wow, he'd been on the receiving end of a woman's anger many a time, but Bindarra Creek's park ranger was the first to make him feel lower than cockroach droppings. Either she really took her job seriously or she disliked newcomers to their half-awake town, or there was something much, much deeper driving her fury.

He felt like he'd gone ten rounds with Danny Greene and come out of the ring reeling from the punches. Had he just made the biggest mistake of his life? He'd committed career suicide by leaving the city to move to a town where so far, the ride had more downs than the Dow Jones during the GFC. What was he thinking? What did he know about kangaroos and country pubs? Jesus, he barely knew how to pour a beer let alone pull one. *Way to go, Molyneaux.*

Alice opened the driver's side door and got in behind the wheel. She pulled on her seatbelt and started the engine. He wanted to ask if everything was okay but he figured he'd be better off keeping his mouth shut. She must have felt his quick glance on her face because she cast him a look offside.

"The joey's fine. No broken bones and he's dealing with the shock well enough to have a drink. Lucky, he's a little older so his chance of survival without his mum is higher," she said quietly.

"Thanks. It helps to know that." Dan sensed that most of the fight had gone out of her, but judging from her pale cheeks and red-rimmed eyes, whatever had got her going still simmered close to the surface.

"Here." She tossed him a sample bottle of antiseptic hand gel. "Use this to clean your hands. You don't want to get sick. Roos carry a number of germs that aren't pleasant when transferred to humans. There's a tub of wipes at your feet to clean away the blood first."

Great, he thought as he leaned forward to do as she instructed.

They drove in silence back onto Main Street and turned onto Mt Ingalls Street, where he knew Mum had bought an old cottage. The small town grapevine must have let her know they were on their way because there she stood, waiting at the gate with a wooden spoon in her hand.

Dan grinned, the dark cloud lifting a little. Baking was what Mum did when she was worried. God bless her, he hoped that spoon had whipped up a batch of scones and wasn't meant for whipping his arse! She'd had to use a few for the latter in his younger days. He'd grown up better for it.

The months away from the city had been good to her. Although her hair was greyer now, there was a sparkle in her eye and colour in her cheeks he hadn't seen in Sydney. It looked like Bindarra Creek's fresh country air had worked its magic on her. God, he hoped there was some of that magic left over for him.

"This is your stop. Fred will drop off your bags when he tows the car in," murmured Alice as she drew to a halt outside the gate and waved to his mum.

"Thanks for the ride."

"No worries."

Not *it's a pleasure, welcome to town*, just *no worries*. Dan wanted to say more, but his tongue had cleaved to the roof of his mouth and his throat choked around what to say. She turned to roll down her window and greet his mum, while he opened the door and got out.

"Alice, honey, Fred called to tell me where you picked Dan up. Are you okay, love?"

"I'm fine, Maureen, thanks for asking. It was bound to happen sooner or later. Driving past is one thing, having to stop is something else, but I can deal with it. I have to. It's my job."

As Dan stepped onto the pavement, he saw the flicker of pain in Alice's green eyes. He pecked a kiss on his mum's cheek and she pulled him in for a hug with her arm around his waist.

"It's good to have you home, Dan," she said, pressing her cheek against his chest as he dropped a casual arm around her shoulders. "Alice, would you like to come in for a cup of tea and a scone? I have some fresh fig jam for them."

Alice's gaze slipped to Dan's face, then flicked away again. "Thanks, but I'll have to pass. I need to get the carcass to the butchery. There might be enough left to render it for the dogs."

Dan squirmed at the thought. Better than leaving

it to the meat ants and other scavengers on the side of the road, he guessed.

"Righto then," Maureen said and squeezed Alice's elbow where it lay on the open window. "Thanks for bringing Dan home."

"Sure."

She turned to face the windscreen, her eyes on the road ahead and Dan thought she looked like she wanted to make a quick getaway.

"Yeah thanks, Alice."

She nodded. "I'll drop off the keys to Riverside in the morning. Follow Main Street all the way until just before the bridge. You'll see the pub on the right-hand side." Her voice broke on the last word and she swallowed hard enough that Dan could see her throat work. "See you later."

Dan frowned as she drove away and his mum dropped her arm from his waist. "I feel like I've made a mistake coming here." He let her turn out from under his arm and followed her up the pathway to the house.

"Of course you haven't. What makes you think you have?" She pulled open the painted metal flyscreen and waved him inside.

The cool of the air conditioning chilled his skin as he followed her down the hall, past the lounge room with its faded wallpaper behind her favourite armchair, and into the old kitchen where the smell of freshly baked scones teased his senses.

"The accident, the roo, the pub, Alice—" He shrugged. "Signs all pointing to this being a bad idea."

Maureen sighed heavily. "Sit down, Dan. I'll make you a cup of tea and then I'll fill you in on a few of the skeletons in Bindarra Creek's closet."

CHAPTER TWO

*S*keletons. *No kidding*. He was looking at one right now. The walk through town from Mum's place had revealed a few more business tragedies exactly like this one—for sale signs and empty shopfront windows—leaving him in no doubt that Bindarra Creek was a town struggling to stay alive. The Riverside Pub stood silent and deserted under sun's rays that promised another dry, warm day.

Standing in what once might have been a bustling car park, Dan tossed the heavy brass key in his palm as he eyed the peeling lattice on the upper level of his pub. The iron roof would once have been a vibrant red, but now all that remained was the odd stubborn streak of paint and blotches of brown rust.

At least the two chimneystacks looked stable, not that he could say the same for the wooden veranda posts.

Colourful graffiti sprawled across the red brick walls, and some clown had drawn a monkey's arse around the brass doorknob. Dan chuckled. He'd have done the same given the dent in the middle of it made it look like balls. Green paint flaked off the solid wooden door and old, out-of-date posters had faded and torn on the walls between the windows.

If the outside looked this bad, what the hell waited for him inside? With a sigh, he walked across the bitumen to the side of the building and pushed through the dilapidated wooden gate into what once would have been an impressive beer garden. Waist-high weeds to the left had him wondering if it harboured any surprises in the form of snakes—or maybe even lions and tigers. He made his way to the rear on the concrete path, and wished he hadn't as he walked around the corner of the building right into the barrel of a gun.

"Jesus!" He swore and stepped back, hands in the air.

"Freeze, motherfucker!" The gun trembled in the hands of an old man with a gnome-like beard, his head engulfed in a battered bucket-shaped hat two sizes too big. His flannel checked shirt had seen better days and his brown corduroy pants were tied at the waist with ratty leather belt. "Who the hell are you?"

Great, he was being held at gunpoint by Papa Smurf with a bright orange gun that shot foam bullets. "Dan Molyneaux. This is my pub."

"Prove it. Place has been empty for years. We've had lots of trouble with them developers trying to weasel in on these old properties. How do I know you're not one of them? It's not yours until Alice says it is and proves who you are. Where is Alice?"

"Alice, Alice, who the fuck is Alice?" squawked the white and yellow cockatoo as it flew off the man's shoulder and strolled up to explore the laces of Dan's Nikes.

Dan pressed the fingers of one hand to his eyes and kept the other in the air. Could this get any crazier? Not for the first time in twenty-four hours, he wished he was back in his corner office on the thirtieth floor of metropolitan hell where things were normal and he wasn't out of his depth.

"Look, um?" Dan waved a hand towards the toy gun.

"Jake."

"Jake. Alice dropped off the keys at Mum's this

morning. She did mention she had a caretaker looking after the place. So I guess that's you, right? I'm Maureen Molyneaux's son and I arrived in town yesterday. I own the pub. I have the deeds at home if you need proof."

"Ah! Didn't think you'd come by so soon after writing off the roo," said Jake, lowering the gun.

Dan breathed and dropped his raised hands to his hips. "No point in delaying now I'm here."

Jake stepped forward and held out his hand. "Folks around here call me Old Man Jake, and that mongrel bird is Curly."

"Hello," said Curly and pooped on Dan's shoe.

Shit, seriously? Dan gave his foot a shake in an attempt to dislodge the bird and the poop from his shoe, but neither were about to move in a hurry.

"Mmm, I guess Curly likes you then. He doesn't do that to just anyone."

Jake's toothless grin didn't do much to ease Dan's irritation. He swiped a hand through his hair and grunted. "Can't exactly say I feel honoured," he grizzled. "So Alice says you stay on the property?"

"Yeah." Jake nodded, pulled out a crumpled old handkerchief from his top pocket of his shirt and tossed it to Dan to wipe the poop from his shoe. "Rolled into town on me way through to nowhere,

27

liked the place and stayed. Alice gave me a job looking after the pub so those mongrel kids don't mess the place up."

And look how well that worked out. Dan eyed the green and blue tags on the painted white brick. Even the graffiti artists had their opinion of Jake and Curly. "Right." Dan drew out the word. "So, other than security, what else does your job as caretaker involve?"

Jake shrugged. "Alice just said to keep the kids away from inside. No-one's been in there for a long time. Not even those real estate developers got a look into this one. I was surprised to hear she sold the old place, I tell ya. Thought she'd be happy if they bulldozed the joint."

"Yeah, that's not going to happen." Well, not unless the place was about to fall down, which it might do if the termites had gotten into it. Or maybe it should be knocked down then he could sell the land to the developers.

Doubt edged into his mind again. For a savvy investor, he'd sure gone into this one blind. He'd been so damn desperate to get out of the cut throat investment world he'd signed the offer based on nothing more than his mother's word and gut instinct. But then in all fairness, he'd inherited his investment savvy from Mum, and she hadn't been wrong yet. Maudan Investments had a squeaky clean reputation until the Harris scandal.

Well, he was here now and the ink was dry on the contract, the cooling off period a distant memory. The only choice he had was to step inside the ruins of someone else's life and do the best he could to make this venture work.

It wasn't about the money—he had plenty of that —this was a matter of pride, a test that he still had the Midas touch, that he could still function in a business world, that through all the trials of the Harris case, he'd retained at least some of his integrity.

With an amused look at the ancient caravan parked next to the old shed, he assumed that's where Jake and Curly lived. "That yours?"

"Yep," said Jake. "Is it a problem?"

"No, as long as it's safe and there's no gas leaks or anything that will blow up my pub."

Jake snorted. "Wouldn't be staying in it if there was, son."

"Good." He walked up to the back door of the pub, pushed the heavy brass key into the hole and turned. The grating noise as the old lock shuddered and ground open scraped at his nerves. He pushed at the door with his shoulder in the centre and a foot at the base to force it open. Years of rain had soaked into the unprotected wood, swelling it inside the frame. It opened with some persuasion and Dan stepped into the gloomy kitchen.

Dust motes swirled in the murky light coming from the dirt-caked windows, the smell of old oil and grease hung thickly in the air, but what hit him in the stomach with a punch was the air of emptiness, desertion and desolation. Next to him, Jake shivered and Dan figured he must have felt it too.

"Creepy," said Curly as he clawed his way up the leg of Jake's pants. The old man scooped a finger under the bird's claws and transferred him to his shoulder.

Dan certainly couldn't disagree. It was as if Alice truly had turned off the lights, locked the door and left it exactly as it was after the last drink was poured. His fingers searched the wall for a light switch. He wished he'd taken Mum's advice and brought a flashlight as his fingers brushed against years' worth of cobwebs. The ghostly shadows of cooker hoods, prep tables and fridges loomed in the gloom.

He found the switch and flicked it on. Overhead, a handful of fluorescent lights convulsed to life while the rest hummed in vain. Dan sighed as he looked around. The place looked better with the lights off. If his stomach could drop any further he'd be tripping over it with his feet.

Beside him, Jake whistled. "You're going to need a hand cleaning up this mess, mate." He nodded to the industrial cooker hood caked in dust that adhered to the stickiness of old oil. "Might have to get the pest man in first. Those cockroaches have been having a bloody party on that cooker."

Dan sighed. He'd told Alice he'd never killed a cockroach in his life and here he stood looking at an army of the little buggers. Hadn't he read once that they were the only things to survive a nuclear bomb? Shuddering, he headed toward a doorway he guessed would lead into the pub.

The wooden floorboards creaked under his feet as he stepped through and found himself behind the bar area. Sunlight drifted weakly through the gaps in the boards on the windows. Desertion and sadness, deep and gut-wrenching, hung in the air as if the ghosts of past patrons waited around the bar for a drink.

Oh dear God! Get over yourself, Dan. His associates from the corporate world would piss their pants laughing if they could hear his fanciful thoughts now. He dealt in facts and figures, talked up shaky investments and made them look like million-dollar money-spinners. Hard-arsed business called for hard-arsed tactics that didn't involve hearts and flowers. They'd called him Slugger—slug it to 'em and walk away. Then the financial crisis had hit and his clients—Harris in particular—had lost their superannuation investments along with their properties. The day he'd had to take a good long, hard look at himself was one he'd never forget. He hadn't liked what he'd seen.

"Want me to hit the lights?" Jake asked, dragging Dan from his thoughts.

Curly squawked loudly in his ear as he hopped from Jake's shoulder to Dan's. "Lights, lights, fer fuck sake."

Dan grinned. Curly didn't like the dark eerie, damp space any more than he did. "Let's get those boards off the windows to start, I think. Got a hammer, Jake?"

"Yeah, mate. Shed out the back is full of tools. I'll grab 'em for ya." He turned and went back through the kitchen, leaving Curly and Dan to feel their way around.

Dan found the hook under the bar counter right where Alice said it would be. He hitched the heavy ring of keys into his hand and took it across to the window to get some light on the task. Searching through the bunch, he found the one marked for the front door.

"This is it, Curly. I hope the front door opens a little easier than the back one did."

Curly muttered on his shoulder as Dan leaned down to insert the key in the lock and turn the knob. The bird swore as he jerked the door open.

"Seriously, Curly? Is that the only word you know?"

"Shit, shit."

Dan sighed and pulled the door wide, letting in the early morning sun. He tested his weight on the wooden boards before stepping out onto the veranda. They creaked dryly under his feet, but thankfully stayed intact.

As he stepped out of the gloom and into the warm sun, some of the tension slipped from his shoulders, and for the first time since arriving in Bindarra Creek he felt the pull of a challenge in his blood. He'd taken his first steps into the unknown and God it felt good to shake some of the doubt, if not the guilt, that dragged at him.

The animals were fed and watered, and the stalls mucked out. Alice's excuses had run out. She'd delayed her trip to the vet—and the inevitable drive past Riverside—for long enough. Handing over the key to Dan Molyneaux this morning was harder than she thought it would be. If the man had any sense at all, he'd bulldoze and start over, build a shopping hub or a townhouse complex or whatever else investors and developers conned innocent people into— anything other than a pub.

Alice sighed. Instead she'd have to drive past the old pub and watch it transform into someone else's dream. As long as the bastard building stood on the side of the road into town, it would constantly remind her of what she'd lost, of the mistakes she'd made.

The vet had rung to say the joey was okay, but needed a little nurturing, too young to be left on his own. Alice smirked. Well, she'd make that Dan Molyneaux's problem. He'd just become the proud father to a baby joey. No man ran faster than one presented with a baby to look after, furry or otherwise. His city boy manicure and pressed pants would soon be covered in kangaroo shit and grime. How long would his expensive shirts hold out on that?

She tossed the empty little blue sleeping bag in through the open window of the ute then pulled the door open and slid onto the seat next to it. With a sigh, she turned the key in the ignition and put the ute into gear as melancholy settled on her shoulders once more.

Seeing life at the pub again would take some getting used to, and she wasn't at all sure she could do that. Perhaps it was time to move on somewhere else, start over, and leave the ghosts behind. Even as she thought it, she knew she could never relocate from the place where her heart and dreams lay buried. Alice let out the clutch, and the ute moved forward down the gravel driveway of the animal sanctuary onto Main Street.

Slowly crossing the bridge, she cast a look to her left and saw Dan prying the nails from the boards on the windows of Riverside Pub. She shuddered. The transformation had begun and with every nail he removed, each one ripped open her heart, tearing the lid off memories she'd buried deep, forcing her to face her guilt and pain. Right now, she hated Dan Molyneaux with all her heart, even though common sense told her it was irrational.

The wheels of the ute spun on the road as she accelerated too quickly. Alice looked away as Dan turned around, and concentrated on keeping to the speed limit as her body trembled and her hands shook on the wheel.

Dan pried the board loose from the window, spider webs forming a sticky bond to the wooden frame. He propped it up against the wall. What had gotten into Alice? She'd wheel-spun away like he'd threatened her with the crowbar in his hand. Like all women, she confused the hell out of him. If she didn't want to sell the damn pub, why hadn't she just said so? No-one had held a bloody gun to her head to sign the transfer papers.

Sure, he understood her loss. He couldn't imagine losing someone as close as a partner, or a child. Mum had cried a little when she'd told him how Alice had lost her family and how she'd locked her pain away like she'd locked up the pub, and that made him feel an even bigger dick for having the accident where he had.

"Was that Alice?" Jake stepped out onto the veranda with a bucket of hot soapy water in one hand and a squeegee in the other.

"Yeah," Dan said around the nail heads in his mouth.

Jake shook his head. "You'll swallow those nails, son. Spit 'em out." He held out his hand and waited as Dan removed them from his mouth and placed them in his hand. "Did she stop?"

Dan shrugged. "No, not really, slowed down a little." He moved to the next window and eased the crowbar in behind the board, giving it a push.

"Mmm," said Jake, drawing the hum out speculatively.

"Mmm what?" Dan stopped mid-pry, the crowbar wedged between the window frame and board.

Jake grinned. "Well, usually she just drives by like she can't get past quickly enough. Doesn't even look twice. It's hard for her, you coming here and opening the place up."

Dan looked away and continued to work on the window. Give him an investment deal that looked like it was on shaky ground, and he could fix it with a flick of his fingers and a calculator, but fixing women with issues was not his forte. Alice Pritchard would just have to damn well get over it. He'd bought her pub, paid her more than it was worth—from what he'd seen so far—and she could take her half-a-million dollars and relocate if she didn't like him reopening it up again.

"Dickhead, dickhead," squawked Curly.

Dan agreed. Had he said that thought out loud? And how the hell could a bloody parrot make him feel so damn guilty? He turned to see Curly perched on the railing at the end of the veranda, wings spread, body low and sweeping as he hissed and swayed in the direction of two teenage boys walking past.

"Stupid cockhead," called one of the boys.

"Oi! You bloody little mongrels!" yelled Jake. "I'm gonna clobber the pair of you, teaching Curly those swearwords."

Dan held onto Jake's arm and pulled him back as he headed in their direction with his fists in the air. "Whoa there, Papa Smurf. Let it go."

Caps on backwards, singlets under open shirts and feet in bush boots, the boys were all attitude, testosterone and boredom. He'd bet his last dollar these two were the artists who'd decorated his side wall with insults. Just like city kids, all the entertainment in the world would not keep them out of trouble when they hit the streets and flexed their smarts.

"Hey, I'm Dan," he called out. "Where you boys off to?"

"What's it to you?" The taller of the two pushed his cap up.

Dan placed his hands on his hips and stared the boy down. With a flinch, the kid swivelled his cap the right way around and dragged it down to shade his eyes.

"I hope you boys aren't going to make mischief over the bridge at the sanctuary. Alice has had enough trouble there lately." Jake stepped up beside Dan. "Hen's eggs go missing and end up smashed on her roof the minute she goes out."

"That's not cool, fellas." Dan stepped off the veranda and strode toward them. "How about I give you a clean-up job instead?"

A look passed between the boys as Dan waited. With a shrug, the taller of the two said, "Yeah, okay. What's it pay?"

"Well, you see, I'd like to get the wall down the side of the pub repainted. Alice doesn't need to see the filth written on it every time she drives past." He stroked the day-old stubble on his chin. One of the perks of not having to dress up for the office was he didn't have to shave if he didn't feel like it. Perhaps he could be a country boy after all. "How about it, boys? I'll pick up some paint and you two can come back tomorrow and cover it up."

With a smirk, Lanky twisted the peak of his cap to the side in line with his cheek. "I have two words —" He pulled out a can of red spray paint and wrote *fuck you* on the gravel at Dan's feet, then the two turned and walked back in the direction they came from.

"Cocky little shits," muttered Jake, ready to follow them, waving the crowbar in the air.

Dan caught the back of his shirt in a fist and pulled him back. "Let them go, Jake. They'll keep. If nothing else, we stopped them spray painting the eggs red or whatever else they had planned for that can. Speaking of Alice—"

"Alice, Alice, who the—"

Dan turned to the bird who hopped up and down the veranda rail. "Don't say it, Curly, or I'll deliver you to the closest taxidermist."

"Whaaaaa," Curly squawked.

Jake cackled. He waved down the street to where Alice was driving towards them, blowing the horn as the two boys played chicken in the road in front of her. "Hope she smacks those bloody little mongrels around the ears."

Dan watched the boys jump out the way as Alice

slowed down to give them a mouthful. Whatever she said to them, they had the good grace to drop their heads and scuff their shoes on the gravel before she pulled away from them again. His heart did a little dance in his chest as she headed towards the pub and slowed down again. Through the windscreen he saw her, hair tied back in a ponytail, face free of cosmetics, and her face set seriously. In that moment he realised how much he'd like to see her smile—a real smile—one that lit her face and put the sparkle back in her eye. Only God knew why he'd want that, but his heart agreed while his mind pushed the thought away. Then his errant heart took a dip into his stomach.

"Holy shit, she's stopping," said Jake, his voice filled with awe.

CHAPTER THREE

*A*lice saw Dan and Jake standing at the side of the road as she braked to pull over. Her heart raced as she saw they'd removed a few boards from the windows. Pain choked her throat and she blinked away the tears that stung her eyes. *For God sake, get over it,* she urged herself. Seeing the building come to life again was something she'd have to get used to. Maybe it was time to move the animal sanctuary across town, closer to the vet perhaps.

She pushed the gearstick into neutral, pulled up the park brake and turned off the engine. For a moment she sat, taking short sharp breaths to control the rush of anxiety she felt every time she passed the place. The attacks had increased since she'd signed the sale documents. Would they ever go away? Her hand shook on the handle as she forced herself to push the door open.

"Hey, Alice."

Dan was there, his hand on the door to hold it open as she got out. She tried to pry a greeting from her lips, but they glued firmly shut as her throat closed. Her palms and forehead dampened with perspiration. She swayed as her vision darkened, her head whirled and her mind called for her to breathe.

His hand touched her shoulder, firm but gentle. "You okay? You look a little pale."

Alice kept her eyes on her boots. *In, out, in, out,* she chanted silently. *Don't think about what happened that night. Think about the joey.* Fear—tangible, cold and unreasonable—crept up her spine. From a distance, she heard Old Jake mutter something, but she couldn't make out the words for the buzz in her ears.

"Alice?" Dan's hands steadied her as she rocked forward. "What's wrong?"

She shook her head. The world swam around her as her knees buckled. Strong arms swept her up. Alice wanted to protest, to push away, but her muscles wouldn't obey. Instead, she clutched at Dan's T-shirt, closed her eyes and buried her face against his chest. Dan was moving fast. She could feel every bounce in his step. He sat with her balanced on his lap and cradled her close, an arm around her and a hand stroking her hair.

"It's okay, Alice. Breathe, small, easy breaths. Jake's gone to get water. It's all good, honey."

Eyes squeezed shut, she moved to bury her nose in his neck, Alice let the velvet tones of his voice wash over her. She concentrated on the rise and fall of his breathing and patterned hers to match, the constriction in her throat easing. His words continued to soothe while his hands gently eased away the tension in her muscles.

"I'm sorry," she whispered against his skin, not sure if she was apologising to him or to the family she'd lost.

The hand stroking her hair dropped away. "Feeling better?"

She nodded and released her death-grip on his shirt, shifting her face from his neck and resting her cheek against the soothing beat of his heart. Just one more minute, one more moment of not feeling guilty to be alive when everything she had to live for was gone.

"I've got you a glass of water, mate," Old Man Jake's leathery features came into view, his hat tilting loosely on his head.

Dan took the glass and held it to her lips. Alice sipped the tepid tap water, the slightly brackish taste distracting her thoughts as she gained control of her emotions. She pushed the glass away with a "Thank you," and wriggled off his lap.

Her knees wobbled as she stood, realising they were seated on the pub veranda. It was the closest she'd come to the place in almost eight years and it was hard not to stare at the peeling paint or feel the air of desertion that hung over it, the sadness that squeezed her heart. The pressure of fingers against her flesh chased the flashbacks in her mind. She looked up as Dan stood steadying her with a hand on her arm.

"You okay now?"

She nodded. "Yeah. Oh no, the joey!" How could she have forgotten all about the joey on the front seat of her ute? Panic rose again. The heat inside the cab would be climbing with engine and air conditioning turned off. If the joey got too warm, the fluctuation in temperature could kill him. Then she'd have another baby's death on her hands. She turned and started out for the ute.

"Don't worry, love," said Jake, walking towards her with the joey in his arms and Curly on his shoulder. "I've got the little guy."

He placed the fleecy blue pouch in her outstretched arms, and Alice cradled it close, peeking inside to check the joey, reaching in to touch his skin. Relief flooded her as she felt his body temperature—normal. Too hot or too cold and he'd stress out. Instead, he peered at her with drowsy eyes before settling back down to snooze.

The warm press of Dan's chest against her as he looked over her shoulder reminded her that no matter how solid and secure his arms had felt around her, she was here for one reason only—the bundle in her own. She stepped away from him.

"Thanks, Jake." Turning to Dan, she said, "I need your help looking after him for a while. He needs to be fed every couple of hours and I've got my hands full up at the sanctuary at the moment. I've got formula and bottles in the ute, compliments of the vet. I'll need to take him back in for a check-up in a couple of days. Keep him warm and in the pouch. I'll show you how to toilet him. You'll have to do it every two to three hours—" Alice knew she was running on, but as long as her mouth was moving, she didn't need to think.

"Whoa, back up, Mack truck." Dan stepped back with his hands in the air. "I can barely keep a pot plant alive, let alone a wild animal. You want me to write up his investment portfolio and plan his retirement fund—I'm your man—but feeding a kangaroo from a bottle and mixing up formula? No way."

"You killed his mother."

"It was an accident!"

"You owe it to him."

"What?" Dan stepped towards her. "How?"

Alice stuck out her chin and looked up, squinting against the sun. "By giving it your best shot so he can go back into the wild."

"I can't!"

"You can." She held the bundle out against his chest. "Take him."

"No!"

"Yes!" Alice gripped his wrist and dragged his arm down to cradle the joey in it then brought his other arm around for support. She stepped away. "Congratulations, you're a father. I'll get his things."

Without giving him time to respond, she walked to the ute, dragged out a cardboard box and loaded it into Jake's waiting arms. Then she made the mistake of looking back.

Her heart hitched as she watched Dan peer into the pouch, a grin pulling at his mouth. The sunlight behind him picked out the lighter shades of his dark brown hair, cut short, ruffled by his hands and the breeze. His eyes, when she'd looked into them earlier, were the deep, dark brown of chocolate flecked with hazel. But it was his lips that drew her gaze now, curved and full, the dance of his mouth as he formed whispered words to the joey like a father bonding with a newborn. Words Pete might have whispered to Lochie if he'd had the chance.

An ache dragged at her heart, far removed from the one that usually clenched it tight. No, this ache didn't feel like loss, it felt like an awakening, and she wasn't having a bar of it.

Dan eyed the joey, which looked back unblinkingly. Okay, so the little guy was cute, but caring for him twenty four hours a day, seven days a week was stretching the friendship. When would he ever get any work done around the place? A man couldn't have a joey in his arms and wield a crowbar at the same time, for God's sake.

"It's not going to work, little guy, sorry." He touched the joey's paw, found it a little too cool and tucked it back into the blue baby pouch. "I'm sure someone else will take you in." The joey burrowed down in the blanket and curled into Dan's chest. "Oh come on now, that's a bit unfair," he said, his tone softening.

"Great, you're bonding," said Alice as she moved outside his personal space and turned toward the ute. "The vet has written down a few instructions for you. I'll show you the basics and leave you to it."

"Wait—"

Her fiery gaze slammed into his, daring him to argue. So Alice thought she had him fooled by her false bravado. He read the pain behind the fire—the embarrassment, the insecurity, the self-doubt and the guilt that caused an anxiety attack. God knew, he'd felt it himself often enough.

"We'll cut a deal, I'll take care of Muttley here if you'll tell me what's up your nose."

Alice slapped her hands onto her hips and puffed out her chest. "*What?*"

Dan shrugged. "What's with the anxiety attacks, Alice?"

"He'll need one level scoop of formula to fifty mils of boiled warm water. He weighs seven kilos, so he'll need seven hundred mils shared into four meals a day."

"When did they start?" Dan moved closer.

Alice wrapped her arms around her waist. "To

toilet him, you'll need to stimulate his glands by applying a soft damp tissue to his bottom."

"How long have you been having the attacks?"

"You'll need to do that before and after feeds. Any problems and you can ring the vet or come over to the sanctuary immediately."

"Have you seen someone about it, Alice?"

"An esky makes the perfect bed. The insulation helps maintain their body temperature. When you feed him, hold him like a baby and then put him back in the esky to sleep."

Dan narrowed his eyes and studied her face, his hold on the joey tightening. It seemed she was quite the expert at evasion, and God help him, he knew what that was like. When inexplicable anxiety gripped your throat and squeezed the air from your lungs until your legs became paralysed with fear and lack of oxygen—he knew that feeling too.

"Okay, you win. Is there a number I can reach you on in an emergency?"

"Jake has it." She turned to walk away. "Thanks for taking care of him."

"Like I had a choice," muttered Dan, watching the sway of her hips as she made her way to the ute. "Hey, Alice?"

She stopped, but didn't look back. "Yes?"

"If you need a friend, someone to talk to about those panic attacks—"

Alice turned and bore down on him with long strides, considering her legs were so short. She leaned in as close as she could with the joey between them. "We made a business deal. You bought the pub and its contents. I'm not included in the price. If I had my way, you wouldn't be in Bindarra Creek because I don't want you here. Like I don't want that pub reopened, but you're going to do it any way. Let's make one thing clear, I am *not* your new best friend."

Her eyes flashed fire, her cheeks rosied up, and the words ground out through perfect white teeth and very kissable lips. Every nicely enunciated syllable punched Dan squarely in the gut and made him feel like an absolute arsehole.

"Ouch," said Jake from the safety of the veranda as she walked away.

Alice controlled her breathing as she checked for traffic then let out the clutch and accelerated onto the road. God damn Dan Molyneaux for turning her world upside down. Who the hell did he think he was? And as for Grandad Charlie—talking her into selling the pub, into moving on when she was content in her comfort zone taking care of the animals that needed her and never asked for more than she was able to give. Why couldn't the people of Bindarra Creek simply accept she was happy as she was?

She pulled into the driveway across the bridge from the Riverside Pub and stopped outside the ramshackle cottage she and Charlie lived in, a fibro relic from the fifties. She'd snapped up the property after leaving the pub. Once an abandoned farm, she'd turned it into an animal sanctuary, a place where she could nurture and love, unlike she'd been able to raise her own family. Between them, she and Charlie had grown a sustainable veggie patch and a rose garden that cheered up the beds lining the outer walls of the house.

A gust of wind blew through the gum trees and the leaves rustled in the breeze. Across the dirt road and into the paddock, she spotted Charlie feeding the alpacas. She'd found them abandoned on the farm when she'd bought it, roaming free, weak and hungry. Her heart softened, pouring soothing oil on her anger. When she'd lost Lochie and Pete, Charlie was all the family she'd had left.

He looked up and waved so she wandered over, taking her time to let the bad mood seep out of her soul. Charlie didn't deserve to bear the brunt of her anger.

"Hey, Pop." She dropped a kiss on his leathery cheek.

"Hey yourself. How'd you go dropping off the little fella?"

Alice shrugged. Across the river above the gum trees, the faded roof of the pub reflected the rays of the sun in a heat-hazed halo. "As well as can be expected, I guess. Stopping was hard. Getting out of the ute was harder. It doesn't feel right."

"What doesn't feel right?"

"It feels like betrayal—the sale, the city boy opening it up again. Maureen says he wants it up and running within a month for Christmas." She tipped her chin in the direction of the pub. "There's a part of me that hopes he won't pull it off in time."

Christmas, she hated the festive season. Each decorated tree, every bloody jingle bell, every carol sung in Memorial Park on Christmas Eve—all of it reminded her of what she'd never celebrate with her family, the child she'd never hold. So every year when they broke out the Aussie Christmas carols and decorated the arches at the park, Alice would find an excuse to escape to the mountains until it was over. Camping under the stars, eating cold beans from a can and sharing the bush with the poisonous brown snakes was a far more attractive way to pass the time.

"It'll be good to see the place come alive again, Al, you'll see."

"Will it, Pop? How long do you think it will be before someone else wraps himself around a damn tree because he's had too many drinks there?"

"You can't control people's choices, child. You certainly can't control dickheads who drink and drive."

"I know, but still, it's not right someone else gets to live Pete's dream. Not when it's my fault he's dead." Alice folded her arms over the fence and rested her chin on them.

"Oh come on, Al. The accident wasn't your fault. There was nothing you could do to stop him getting behind the wheel that night."

"No, but I provoked him, annoyed him, nagged until he cracked. If only I could take back what I said, they might still be alive."

Charlie pulled her into a hug. "My precious child, you have got to stop blaming yourself. You've paid your penance over and over these last eight years. It's time to let go of the past and look to the future."

"How can I have a future when I shouldn't be alive?"

"Alice, my sweet, you're not alive, you're existing."

CHAPTER FOUR

*M*aureen slid the steaming mug of coffee across the table towards him. "What's going on in that head of yours, Daniel?"

Dan sighed as he looked around his mum's kitchen with the scarred Baltic pine cupboards and ancient Formica table, searching for a way to answer. He'd known his mum wouldn't avoid the reason for him coming to Bindarra Creek for long. She'd want to get to the bottom of it, deep beneath what the papers had reported and what he'd told her over the phone. He was surprised she'd left it this long.

Even though he wanted to tell her it was nothing, he knew better than to deny it when she took that no-nonsense tone. He respected her too much. A single mum, she'd raised him alone, worked long and hard at running her own broking business, and turned it into a multi-million dollar empire they'd both benefitted from—until money no longer mattered because it cost lives.

"Why wouldn't you let me come to Sydney and support you through the media storm?" She took the seat across from him and waited. Mum was good at that, the waiting.

"Why drag you down with me?" He raked a hand through his hair. "You'd retired and I was the only remaining shareholder in the business. It was my problem to own. I created it, I had to fix it."

Maureen sighed and took a sip of her coffee. "I get that, and I'm glad you made the decision to sell the business, to get out—but right out of town? You loved Sydney—the life, the rush."

Dan shrugged. "Long hours, long lunches, plenty of money and toys eventually take its toll on a man."

"Bullshit. Try again."

"I had several billion dollars-worth of reasons on my desk in various forms of monetary investments that either killed or bankrupted people. I looked in the mirror and didn't like the man I saw there anymore."

"You blame yourself, don't you? Dan, no-one saw that storm coming and nothing you could have done would have stopped the damage to that development. Darryl Harris was an old hand at playing investments, even back in my day. Hell, he played cards, the horses, the property market and anything else that could be played. He knew what he was doing."

Dan tilted his head to check on the joey, lying peacefully asleep in the hammock under the window where the sun stroked his fur. "I could have stopped it before he signed the papers."

"Dan, I'll only say this once—you are not responsible for the choices Darryl Harris made. You're a man, not God. It's time to forgive yourself and start over. You and Alice are quite the pair, blaming yourselves for the choices people make. It was her husband Pete's choice to get behind the wheel angry, in the rain, on a dangerous road. It was Harris's choice to jump from the roof of an office building. Neither of you can change that." Maureen stood and walked around the table to hug him. "And if I know you well enough—which I do—I'd know you helped his family, right?"

"I set up a trust fund for the kids, but it will never be enough to bring their father back."

"You can't change the world, my darling. You can only do as much as you can to help those in it. I'm glad you're here. This place will be good for you. It's full of people who blame themselves for the actions others have taken. You can help each other get over it."

Dan grinned wryly as she ruffled his hair then bent to kiss the joey. "Yeah, thanks."

"I love you, son. Your dinner is in the oven, roast beef and potatoes. I'm off to play bingo at the RSL club. And Dan?"

He looked up as she slipped on a light jumper to ward off the evening's summer breeze. "Yeah?"

"Go easy on Alice, okay? I heard about her anxiety attack. She took a big step forward stopping by the pub today."

Dan wrapped the warm, clean, fed joey in the pouch and placed him gently on the sofa next to him as he stretched out to watch whatever was on telly. Mum was off socialising, and he was left holding the baby —literally. Great, he could hang out in his boxers, fresh from the shower and not bother with a shirt.

"What do you feel like watching, Muttley?" Dan flicked through the channels—all three of them. "Not much choice, is there?"

The joey squeaked and burrowed deeper into the pouch, eyes drifting closed. Dan rubbed the soft fur on Muttley's ear. After Alice had left the pub, he and Jake had fashioned a hammock from an old pillowcase and hung it on the doorknob for the joey to rest in while they worked. So far, foster parenting wasn't as hard as he'd expected. Muttley's baby quirks were amusing, but it was the bleak look in Alice's eyes that haunted his thoughts.

Her panic had struck him deep. What had happened at the pub to cause an anxiety attack so severe it had all but crippled her? It was his own reaction that stunned him still—the whoosh of protectiveness that had taken him by surprise, the desire to comfort and hold her close, that gut-deep need to reassure her it would be okay because she wasn't alone anymore—he'd never felt any of that as strongly as he had today.

Dan picked up his phone, her number burned into his mind. In case he needed assistance with Muttley, he'd assured himself, but his heart knew differently. Less than two days in Bindarra Creek and his hard edge had begun to fade fast. Blame it on the country air, he thought as he punched in Alice's mobile phone number.

"Bindarra Creek Animal Sanctuary, Alice Pritchard speaking."

He shivered as her soft, velvety voice washed over him despite the cautiously neutral tone. "Hey, Alice, it's Dan."

"It's late."

He glanced at the time on his Hilfiger—9.00 pm. "Sorry, hope I didn't wake you up." Her snort made him smile. "Thought I'd let you know Muttley's doing fine."

"You seriously named the joey?"

The mixture of resignation and surprise in her voice stretched his smile to a grin. "Yeah well, you know—hey, he took all his feed tonight and now we're looking for something to watch on telly."

"Dan, he's a roo not a dog. Don't get too attached. He has to go back into the wild."

"Yeah, I know, but I might as well make him comfortable while he's here, right? Curly fancies himself a bit of a guard dog now. Jake made a hammock so Muttley can rest while we work and Curly stands guard, lets us know when he wakes up."

"Slotted right in, haven't you?"

Dan heard the slice and ignored it. "Jake's a cool

guy. Got stuck in to give me a hand today. Knows his way around tools at least."

"Dan, I'm busy. I don't have time to chat. Was there anything else you needed to tell me about the joey?" Ice edged into her tone.

"No, but tell me what you know about Lanky and Slim." Dan rubbed a hand over his eyes. It had been a full on day and even with the chill in her, talking to Alice relaxed him. He liked the sound of her voice. Warmed up it would be like hot fudge pudding and custard on a cold night.

"*Who?*"

Okay, annoyance edged with tiredness—time to cut the crap before she put the phone down on him. "The two boys who redecorate your house and roof when you go out? The same ones who spray paint colourful invectives on the side wall of my pub."

Her long sigh coursed through him. He imagined her breath on his ear, sighing with pleasure rather than irritation. Damned if the bristly park ranger hadn't snagged his attention. He put an arm behind his head and rested it against the back of the sofa. Alice was quiet for so long, he thought she might have hung up. He checked the screen just in case. Nope, she was still there.

"So?" he prompted.

"Two bored kids with nothing better to do. There's not much in the way of entertainment in Bindarra Creek for those stuck between childhood and adult. The worst they've done is stolen a few eggs."

"And?"

She sighed again. "Used them to paint the hen house, but—"

Dan chuckled.

"It's not funny. Do you know how hard it is to get egg cleaned up? What do you care anyhow, City Boy? It's none of your business."

Dan pulled Muttley closer into the curve of his body. "I guess I just want to know what I'm up against when I see them next." He wanted to keep her talking, but with the joey asleep peacefully, he'd run out of excuses. "Hey, Alice?"

"Yes, Dan?"

"Sweet dreams." It came out huskier than he'd intended with the image of her in his head, of the vulnerability she'd pushed away earlier today with the stiffening of her spine.

What was it about Alice Pritchard that had his temperature rising, and why in God's good name would a girl so beautiful bury herself in a backwater town so far off the main highway, it was merely a blip on the satellite map?

Alice hung up and shivered. God damn the city boy for having such a sexy voice that it raised gooseflesh on her arms. She tossed the phone onto the yellow countertop and flicked the switch on the kettle. Coffee, that would stop her hands shaking.

"Who was that, love?"

Grandad Charlie walked into the kitchen, trying to mask his limp. The tough old bastard refused to use his walking stick, no matter how much she nagged him. "Mr Mega Investor himself. Have you taken your arthritis tablets?"

Charlie grinned. "Now, my sweet, you go easy on him. He seems a nice young bloke."

"And how would you know? You haven't even met him yet." Alice dropped a teabag in Charlie's cup and heaped a spoonful of coffee into her own.

"Jake says so."

"All hail Saint Jake," muttered Alice.

Charlie laughed and drew the big cup of black tea toward him. "He didn't even flinch when Jake held him at gunpoint with his plastic gun, or when Curly swore a blue streak."

"Give the man a medal!" She scooped two spoons of sugar into her coffee.

"You won't sleep tonight," Charlie warned.

Alice knew that. Her mirror reminded her every morning by showing her the blue-black smudges under her eyes for lack of it. She hadn't slept a wink since the deal on the pub had been finalised and raised her bank balance by enough for a round-the-world trip five times over. Yet here she was, where she'd always been, feeling like she always had—guilty and grieving.

"How was bingo?"

Charlie shrugged. "Same as every week. Maureen has a mean winning streak." He sipped his tea quietly for a moment. "She's very proud of her boy."

Alice waited, knowing there'd be more to come. There always was. Ever since Maureen had heard Dan was coming to town, the length of Main Street had been regaled with stories from his childhood. And to be fair, she'd smiled at a few of them herself. "Come on, Pop. Spit it out. I have to be up early in the morning."

Charlie lifted rheumy eyes to hers and Alice couldn't help the tug of sadness on her heart. Pop was aging fast. He worried too much—about Bindarra Creek, about the people, but mostly, he worried about her not having rebuilt a life for herself too long after Pete and Lochie's deaths. They'd only had each other for so long now and when he was gone, she'd have no-one.

"Give him a chance, Al. That's all I ask."

"I hope you and Maureen aren't planning a little matchmaking on the side." She tried to keep the warning in her tone gentle. Every time a newcomer came to town, Pop got his hopes up that she'd bury the memories and start over. There was no way in hell she'd let it happen, not even for the grandfather who'd raised her.

"An old man can hope. I wouldn't mind seeing me a great-grandchild before I go."

"You're too stubborn to die and there won't be a great-grandchild any time soon, so you'd better keep letting Maureen win at bingo and stay alive, Pop. I need you around."

"I don't let Maureen win," Charlie protested.

Alice raised an eyebrow at him and pursed her lips.

"Okay, okay, maybe once in a while. It makes her happy." He grinned.

"I'm sure there's a law against that." She leaned over and kissed his cheek. "Don't stay up too late."

"Hey, Al?" He watched her walk to the kitchen door, pausing in the frame. "Don't you think you've punished yourself for long enough?"

Alice shook her head. "A lifetime isn't enough." She caught the hitch in her throat and swallowed it back. "Nothing I do will bring them back, I know that. I just haven't found a good enough reason to find a life without them."

"Ghosts won't warm you in winter or keep you company on lonely nights forever, Al. Pete wouldn't want it that way."

"I know. Night, Pop, I'll see you in the morning before I start my rounds."

Alice closed her bedroom door and leaned back against the hard wood. Pete with the cocky grin and cheeky swagger that had won her young heart fifteen years ago—God, she'd loved him with all her teenage being. But he'd been angry, resentful, always so angry at life in a small town, always searching for a way to leave. She'd thought she could fix that by being a good wife and friend. It hadn't taken long for their dreams to crumble.

Dan thought a stroll down Main Street would be a good way to clear his head after a restless night. The joey had slept like the proverbial baby between feeds, but Dan had found his head full of Alice.

According to the town grapevine, the car crash, the death of her husband and losing her baby only two months before he was due, had sent her spiralling into depression. She'd not only closed the doors of the pub, she'd closed the door on life. It seemed such a pity, such a waste that she'd shut out the world.

In the sling across his chest, the joey wriggled and squeaked. Dan adjusted the inner pouch as the joey poked its head out for a sniff at the morning air.

"Looking pretty good, isn't it, Muttley? Morning, ladies."

He waved to the huddle of elderly women outside the newsagent's. The Country Women's Association had worked hard to lure life back to the dying town, according to Mum. He hoped they succeeded or he'd be sitting with an empty pub and a broken bank account.

"Morning," they chorused.

He smiled and wondered if they'd be up for a bit of karaoke when he got things going. They might be his only customers. He added a good port and sherry to the growing stock list in his head, something to warm them up on those wintery country nights.

Approaching the bend in the road past the IGA and the vacant shop where a sign in the window promised something exciting coming soon, he almost walked into the back of a man hobbling in the direction of Riverside.

"Sorry," he said, putting out a hand to steady the startled man.

Dressed in faded denims and a checked shirt, bent and obviously arthritic, the old boy leaned on a cane he pretended not be using and straightened his back as far as he could. "Ah, you must be Dan. How's the joey doing? I'm Charlie, Alice's grandad." He turned and held out his hand for a shake.

"Dan Molyneaux, pleased to meet you."

"Same. I was coming up to see how my old mate Jake is doing. He didn't come to bingo last night."

"That might be my fault." Dan grinned. "He worked hard helping me take all the boards off the windows of the pub yesterday. I think I might have tired him out."

Charlie chuckled. "Probably the most work the old bastard has done in his life." He shook his head. "Old man Jake—no-one really knows where he came from or why. He just showed up in town one day, liked it and stayed. He's been a great help while the pub's been closed. He's kept away the worst of the trouble."

Dan laughed. "Except for the graffiti artists who've decorated the north side wall."

"Yeah, except for them. So, Maureen tells me you're an investment broker."

Charlie's words cut into his soul. He hadn't realised how much he'd regret his career choice until now. There was simply no escape from it, not even in a small town like Bindarra Creek.

Dan adjusted the weight of the joey against his chest. "Not anymore."

"Let's walk. My hip gets sore standing around too long. What made you give it up and move to Woop Woop?"

"The city lights lost their sparkle."

Charlie chuckled. "Who needs lights when out here in the bush you have the moon and the stars, hey? Still, a handsome young fella like you coming to town when the rest your age are leaving? An old man has to wonder, you know."

Dan squirmed under the old man's direct gaze. His eyes might be rheumy, but behind them he could almost hear Charlie's brain ticking over. The man had likely read the news reports, whichever version of it they'd received out here. Like it or not, the grapevine would soon run hot with rumours so he may as well tell the old man what he wanted to know.

"I made a few bad choices and figured if I ever wanted to sleep well at night again, it was time for a career change."

"Mmm," said Charlie, narrowing his eyes. "Not hard to put two and two together, son. Not even for an old man like me. That Harris scandal put a bad taste on many an investor's tongue. Your name was dragged through the shit well and good, but there're three sides to a story as they say, and the media's version isn't always the truth. Here in Bindarra Creek we take care of our own, so be prepared to be questioned until the townsfolk have drained every drop of truth out of your bones."

"I've no doubt," muttered Dan dryly.

"You're Maureen's son—that counts in your favour."

They turned at the crunch of tyres on the road and saw Alice approaching in the ute. She pulled up beside them and rolled down the window.

"Pop! Why didn't you wait for me? I said I'd drop you off at Jake's after I'd done my rounds. Now here you are wandering around town, way past Jake's caravan."

Charlie patted Dan's arm. With a wink, he said, "She's a good girl, my Alice—a dreadful nag but a good girl nonetheless. It's a beautiful morning, young lady, and my legs work just fine, thank you. And I got to have a good chat with my mate Dan here."

"Hi Dan," she said without looking at him. "Get in, Grandad."

Charlie chuckled. "She only calls me that when I'm in trouble. What about a lift for Dan and the joey too then, Al? They've walked all the way from Maureen's place."

Alice snorted. "What, all four blocks? They must be exhausted. Should've called a taxi, City Boy."

Dan's lips twitched at her sarcasm. He liked a challenge. "Well, now you mention it, my feet are a little tired and Muttley's no lightweight, you know."

Alice rolled her eyes. "All right, get in, Desk Jockey. Maybe a few months of country air will toughen you up." Her gaze raked over him, sized him up.

Everywhere her eyes touched, even his cheeks, burned. When her gaze finally came up to meet his, the hazel depths lured him in, set the dare. So he looked back as hard she had, following the curve of her neck, the ponytail over her shoulder, and the vee of her shirt that revealed the promise of a very satisfactory cleavage.

She leaned over to push open the door, her teeth nibbling her lower lip and the pucker of the frown on her forehead. Yep, he'd rattled her and she didn't like it one bit. He, on the other hand, liked it a lot.

"You first, son," said Charlie. "I like to be close to the window."

A deliberate set-up if ever there was one. Dan snorted. Alice's low growl of warning to Charlie let him know she was onto it too, but never one to back down from a challenge, he got in and slid along the bench seat, trying not to squash poor Muttley in the process. The joey squeaked and popped his head out to see what was going on. As Alice's hand moved to the joey's head, he did the same and his hand ended up covering hers. Her fingers—deceivingly tiny and delicate beneath his—flinched at the contact but she didn't withdraw.

Cupped under his palm her skin was soft and warm. Dan thought about threading his fingers through hers and lifting that hand to his lips to taste the softness. How could hands so beautiful be strong enough to lift a kangaroo, shoot a gun? Their eyes shifted and held, the joey forgotten as the spark between them flared.

"Ahem!" Charlie wriggled his hips. "Move up, mate. My butt is a little wider than yours."

And because it made Alice blush a very becoming pink, Dan shifted until his thigh pressed against hers, a leg on either side of the gearshift. She moved her hands back to the steering and focused on the road ahead.

"You're going to have to move your legs or I won't be able to change gears," she said, pointedly.

Charlie chuckled. "Can't see how that would work, love. He's got damn long legs."

Dan straightened his back and shifted so his backside was as far back in the seat as it could be without hitting his head on the roof of the cabin. "Better? It's only a few blocks, Alice."

"Just as well, because we'll be getting there in no higher than third gear," she muttered, giving Charlie a killer glare when he chuckled again.

Dan grinned and leaned down to whisper, "Go easy on me, Ranger. It's my first time."

Alice grimaced as she started the ute and reached across Dan's thigh to select first gear. "If you so much as wriggle, Molyneux, I swear I'll shoot you."

"Yes, ma'am," he teased, his smile stretching as he noticed the twitch of Alice's lips.

Four excruciatingly long blocks later, his smile was frozen on his face as with every brush of her forearm against his thigh when she changed gears, she extracted penance for his sins. Payback was a bitch and Alice knew how to play it for all it was worth. If it wasn't for the joey resting in his lap hiding his reaction, she'd have a damn good reason to shoot him.

CHAPTER FIVE

*A*s the ute rolled to a stop outside the pub, Charlie laughed out loud. "Would you look at that clown?" He pointed to where Jake sat on the veranda, feet up on the rail, the chair tipped back on two legs, hugging a massive plastic orange machine gun. The bitumen in the empty car park was littered with bright blue and orange sponge bullets, and Curly was having a ball playing fetch.

Alice tried hard and failed to avert her gaze from the bared windows as the morning sunlight bounced off them. Next to Jake an upended bucket stood drying while the squeegee was wedged between the flaking pickets of the veranda rail. Gone were the peeling posters and broken plastic frames, leaving the red brick walls bare. Jake had obviously been busy because she could see the difference between the walls he'd pressure cleaned and the ones he hadn't.

Charlie pushed open the door and hobbled out around the hood. "Look at you, you silly bugger! Playing fetch with a parrot..." he snorted, ambling towards the veranda.

When Dan didn't move, she cast him a look that arched her eyebrows. He grinned back at her, ignoring her obvious annoyance.

"Thanks for the lift."

His breath, all minty and fresh, brushed against her cheek. She ignored the flutter it caused in her stomach. "You're welcome."

In an awkward movement, Dan shifted his leg across the gearstick. For a moment his thigh pressed tightly against hers before he completed the move. His hip grazed hers, leaving a warm imprint before the breeze crept into the gap.

"Want to come in and see what Jake's been up to?" Dan shot her an enquiring look over his shoulder.

"No!" The word came out sharply as she snapped her gaze back to the road.

"Okay."

She felt Dan shrug and slide across the seat with

the joey in his lap, the spring in the suspension as he eased himself and the joey out of the ute. The door closed firmly before he ducked down into her peripheral vision and stuck his head back in the window.

"Alice?"

"Dan?" she responded, her tone mocking as she kept her focus on the road ahead.

"You can't avoid the place forever."

She dragged her eyes from the bitumen and let them rest on his in a look she hoped was bored and disinterested.

He held it for a heartbeat then said, "See you around." With a wink and slap of the hand on the open window frame, he turned and walked away.

Alice watched the sway of his hips and the way his jeans hugged his thighs, her heart beating in time with his swagger. With a furious swearword Charlie would take her to task for using, she ground the ute into gear and lurched from the gravel onto the road. Dan Molyneaux was a pain in the arse, even though he had a very, very nice one.

Dan chuckled as he heard Alice crunch the gears.

Oh, he'd put a crack in her ice for sure, and she didn't like it one bit. Maybe Bindarra Creek wouldn't be such a boring place to be after all. The toes of his boots sent little blue sponge bullets rolling in the dirt and Curly raced after them. In the pouch the joey wriggled and stuck out his head.

"Hey, young fella," said Jake as Dan climbed the three steps onto the veranda. "Sleep okay last night?"

"Yeah, thanks. Looks like you've been busy already this morning."

"Ah well, you know. Figured I might as well get a move on. Been wanting to clean it up for a while now."

"Looks good, thanks Jake." Dan pulled the knot of the sling over his head and off his shoulder, placing the joey in the hammock. "Why don't you two sit here and have a chat while I go and see what we can do next?"

"Sounds good. I cleaned up the kitchen sink so we can at least boil a kettle, mate. Hope you don't mind?" Jake shot off another round of foam bullets—pink this time—sending Curly squawking after them.

"Yep, no worries. I might see if I can get the pest man in before we really get stuck into cleaning the kitchen." Dan stepped through the open door.

Under his feet the dust bunnies shivered. With

all the boards off the windows the sun streaked through the clean glass, adding a murky glow. The eerie feeling of desertion lingered but the natural bleed of light had taken the edge off. Was that what kept Alice away—the sadness that seeped through the walls, the heavy silence that hung in the air or the echoes of the past that resounded through the empty room? That was where he needed to begin. He needed the cathartic exorcism of his own personal demons and by clearing out Alice's ghosts, he hoped his would follow.

Energised, he strode to the back wall and snapped on light switches. There were a few dead ones amongst the lights that flickered to life, making it easy for him to identify the ones he needed to replace globes for. He marched through the gritty kitchen, crunching the odd cockroach beneath his boots. Stepping out the back door, he headed for the shed where he hoped to find a ladder. The metal hinges squealed in protest as he dragged the big door open to peer inside.

"Holy fuck!"

The shed was a barn, a massive man cave twice the size of his Gold Coast holiday penthouse that stretched into darkness—okay, maybe not that big but close enough. In awe, he eyed the gym equipment covered in cobwebs, a battered punching bag and a rack of weights stacked against the side wall. And that was just what he *could* see. God knew what the shadows hid, but at least he'd found a place to work out his frustrations. Country life was looking up. It might not be the modern generation, inner city jock's gym he was used to, but it got him a little excited.

Grinning like an idiot, he found the ladder and searched for a store of light bulbs. *Bingo.* He lugged the box over into the pub and returned for the ladder. As he turned back from the shed, he saw it. The whole side wall of the pub was covered in egg splatters.

"I'm going to kill those little shits," he muttered, walking back into the pub.

As Dan moved from light to light replacing the bulbs, he formulated his plan for payback. Lanky and Slim were in for a surprise.

Charlie ambled through the door and watched Dan screw in the last bulb. "Have you seen the living quarters yet, mate?"

Dan looked down at him from the third rung of the ladder. "Second day on the job, Charlie, cut me some slack."

"Mmm," muttered the old man.

Dan sighed and dusted the cobwebs from his hands. Alice's grandad obviously had something on his mind. "Hit the lights then tell me what you're thinking."

"Righto," said Charlie, wandering over to the flick the switch.

A warm glow encompassed the pub turning the shadowy shapes of tables and chairs into a solid presence. Dan took a moment to admire the sturdy jarrah tables. Those he could work with. The plastic outdoor chairs would have to go. He envisioned stools made from the solid trunks of recycled trees—smoothed off and polished—surrounding those scarred tables. He'd recreate the natural touch outside when he got stuck into rehabilitating the forlorn and forgotten beer garden. Catching Charlie's eye as the old man steadied the ladder for him to step down, he saw a flicker of sadness.

"So what's upstairs then," he asked as he climbed off the ladder.

"Memories, very sad memories for Alice."

"I can't imagine anything about the pub wouldn't bring back those sad memories. This must be hard for her."

Charlie nodded. "She's a good girl, my Alice. Just

like her mum. All I ask is that you be gentle with her memories because one day, she'll thank you."

Dan frowned. Why did the elderly always speak in riddles? "What do you mean?"

Charlie shuffled over to the bar and leaned against it, tiredness etched in every wrinkle on his aging face. "She took nothing with her when she locked up the place. Not even her clothes. The poor girl couldn't bear coming back here to sort through it all. After the accident, she never came near the place again." He pushed away and walked over, stopping in front of Dan, toe to toe. "Even I can't bear to go up there. The sadness is too much."

Unease rippled up Dan's spine as he looked across at the solid wooden staircase leading up to the second floor. He wasn't sure he would be comfortable sorting through Alice's personal belongings. Which had him wondering if his mother had known that when she'd sold him on the idea of buying the pub, even promising to work in the kitchen preparing the counter meals. Not that she wasn't a good cook or anything, but her focus until her retirement from Maudan Investments had always been on the monetary side of business.

With a sigh, he folded the ladder and lay it down

on the floor. "What do I need to take extra care with up there?"

Charlie raised sad eyes to his and Dan realised the wateriness in them had nothing to do with the man's age.

"The baby's stuff."

Alice tossed a handful of oats into the goat pen and tried not to think of the upheaval the sale of the pub had caused in her life. And damn Dan Molyneaux for being so *nice*. Why couldn't he be ugly, full of warts, short and lumpy? No, instead he was all broad shoulders, warm chest, slim hips and a hot, feel-worthy arse. She hated how her pulse sped up at the sight of him, and that pull she'd felt when his thigh had skimmed hers. Not to mention what the whisper of his breath in her ear had done for her hormones.

Needy, that's all she was. Eight years was a long time—but his arms had felt so good around her, so warm and comforting, safe and secure. She'd missed that skin on skin contact, that feeling of being loved, held in a man's arms with the beat of his heart against hers. He'd smelled so good—the mixture of shower soap and man.

Guilt tugged at her conscience. She shouldn't be noticing these things. It could only bring heartache. Dan Molyneaux had to stay off limits. She had no need for a man in her life ever again. Best she stayed away.

Her thoughts strayed to how she'd left the living quarters above the pub. Pain stabbed at her heart as her mind's eye skimmed past Lochie's room and moved to the main bedroom. All Pete's stuff still hung in the wardrobe, all her cosmetics would be where she'd left them in the small bathroom. She'd meant to go back, to clear it all out, but the time had never seemed right. And then the panic attacks crept in when she got near the place so she gave up trying. Now a total stranger had control of her past. She should have taken care of it sooner.

Picking up the bucket of food, Alice crossed the path to the kangaroo enclosure. They watched her warily through big round eyes as she approached. She wished with all her heart she had the same courage as a kangaroo, that survival instinct that kept them alive, the strength to get up no matter how badly injured they were, and keep going.

All the animals fed and watered, Alice lifted a hand to shade her eyes from the noonday sun and looked across the river at the roof of the pub. Soon it would be time to fetch Charlie from his visit with Jake and Dan. These days Pop tired quickly, a sign that his heart wasn't getting any healthier. She worried about him, the stubborn old codger. A smile stretched her lips. She didn't want to think about life without him, it was too sad, but as the years marched on it was a reality she'd have to face. When that happened there'd be nothing left to keep her in Bindarra Creek, except for the animals.

Whether she liked it or not, life was moving on without her. The CWA had got their government grant to rebuild the town, people were slowly moving back and Dan was reopening the pub. Alice waited for the pain to spear her heart at the thought. She dropped her hand from her face when it didn't come —that resentment, the ache, the emptiness. Instead her traitorous mind remembered his teasing grin, the twinkle in his green eyes as he'd leaned in through the window of her ute and the cheekiness in his wink. It was so unfair that the city boy could wear his jeans as well as a country boy and look so damn swaggeringly sexy in them.

Even worse, she'd noticed, and liked it.

"Grub's up!"

Dan grinned widely at the picnic basket in his mother's hand. He'd worked hard all morning avoiding taking the stairs to the upper level living quarters. The floor was scrubbed within an inch of its life, the glasses all lined up for washing once the kitchen was disinfected, and anything that looked dead had been turfed in the metal skip bin arranged by Charlie. For an old codger—as he liked to call himself—he sure worked bloody fast when it came to organising things.

Given the interest shown by Slim and Lanky in the liquor bottles being thrown out, Dan had made sure to tip any leftover contents down the loo. If that didn't strip off years of algae in the bowl, nothing would. The two eggheads had strolled by the pub half an hour earlier, their swaggers daring Dan to respond to their egg-throwing skills. He'd resisted, of course—someone had to be the adult here—and ignored them, even though the new-found boy in him wanted to take up arms and riddle them with sponge bullets from Jake's gun.

"Please tell me you have scones and jam in there?" he said, stepping down onto the dirt from the veranda to kiss her cheek.

"I do! And roast beef sandwiches, fried chicken

legs and ice cold beers. I thought you'd all be starving by now." She handed him the basket and dusted off her hands. "It so happens I'm free this afternoon if you need help."

"I hope you brought extra."

Maureen grinned, her smile the perfect mirror for his. "You know I did. Do you think I didn't see Slim and Lanky pretending to fish off the bridge?" She winked at him. "Their real names are John and Tim."

Dan snorted. "Their names won't matter when I'm done with them. Did you see what they've done to the wall with the eggs they stole from Alice?"

Alice's ute crossed the old bridge, stopping for a moment next to the boys, their handlines dangling in the creek.

Speaking of Alice, he watched as she engaged gear and moved forward again, ignoring the increase in his pulse. Would she stop for a bite to eat or would she whisk Charlie away as quickly as she could?

As the vehicle eased to a stop next to them, she dropped her sunglasses over her eyes. She did that well—the hiding thing. He'd done that for weeks too after the press had been focused on his every move following the inquest, until he'd realised that no amount of hiding would take the pain away.

Maureen waved and Alice waved back but didn't make a move to get out. Charlie ambled down the steps and walked over, Jake and Curly close behind.

"Alice—"

"Alice, Alice, who the fuck—"

"Curly!" said Alice and Dan together.

"You're early," continued Charlie with a grin.

"Looks like I'm right on time," she answered. "I've got your favourite on the menu for lunch—cheese toasties."

"Oh."

Dan suppressed a chuckle at the disappointment on Charlie's face. The old man had enjoyed hanging out with him and Jake, telling stories of the days when Bindarra Creek had bustled with prospectors, farmers and town-makers. He'd worked hard at wiping the dust off the tables and taken great delight in tossing the plastic chairs in the skip bin, whistling to himself as he did so.

"I've brought enough for all of us, Alice. Why don't you stay?" Maureen leaned in through the open window to pat her arm.

"I—"

Dan wished she'd take the glasses off so he could read her expression. He didn't like the instant tension in her shoulders and the stiffening of her back. No-one should be that tormented by a building holding memories. He walked around the hood to the driver's side of the cab and leaned down on the open window, his arms crossed, hands tapping at the door panel a touch too close to her arm, holding his own gaze in the reflection of her lenses for a moment.

Shifting, he eased the sunglasses from her face and gently tipped her chin towards him so he could see her eyes. Staring into them, wishing he could read her thoughts, he said, "I'd like you to stay. I need your advice on a troublesome species called *mesolecithal ereptor*. I have a couple hanging out around the place."

"*Mesolecithal*—medium-sized egg thieves?" Alice rolled her eyes and pushed his hand away. "I'll give you the number for our local cop—lay charges. Charlie!"

"Well, I guess there's nothing left for me to do then."

"That's exactly right! Tell a policeman."

Dan grinned, pulled open the door, leaned across to unclip her seatbelt, then scooped her out of the car. "Get the key from the ignition, Charlie. You're staying for lunch."

"Daniel!" Maureen warned.

"Put me down!" Alice squealed.

Dan felt the tension rip through her body, her breath becoming uneven as she squeezed her eyes shut. Remembering the last anxiety attack, he diverted from his initial course from the veranda to under the big bluegum where Jake had left a couple of plastic chairs in the shade. He dropped her gently into a chair and knelt down in the dust, his hands anchored on her shoulders, eyes on her bent head.

"Look at me, Alice. It's okay."

She raised teary eyes to his. "You bastard," she whispered. "I hate you."

"Get in line and take a number, Princess," he said gently as he wiped away a tear with the pad of his thumb. "It's over. You can't ignore it any longer and you won't face it alone. You sold me this pub and I have no choice but to make it work." He cupped her face in his hands, holding her gaze steadily. "I can't do that with your ghosts hanging around."

Alice looked away, fixing her stare on the boys on the bridge. In his peripheral vision, he saw Charlie step forward and Mum put out a hand to stop him.

"Fine then! Set fire to the fucking place for all I care!" Alice choked out. Her leg bounced with pent-up anxiety, her shoulders stiff with restraint. Her face crumpled as she let go of the hurt in her heart.

Dan felt an answering tug. He pulled her off the

chair into his arms and sat in the dirt, holding her securely against his chest as she cried. With his head against hers, he held on until she was spent, and then held on some more, because in each shiver of her body he felt the echo of his own pain and knew it was time for him to let go too.

"Well, look at that...you've made my shirt all damp and snotty. Now I'll have to take it off and expose my magnificent muscles and then you'll be all over me like a rash," he teased.

Alice sniffed. "Don't flatter yourself, City Boy. You don't build muscle pushing pens and lifting briefcases."

"Hey, go easy. I owned a twenty-four-hour gym membership."

"Pfft!"

The huff of her breath reached inside his damp shirt to tickle his skin, and his thoughts took a direction neither he nor Alice were ready for. He loosened his hold on her, giving her the option to move, but she stayed with her head resting on his chest. He leaned back, stretching his arms out behind him, palms in the dirt, and took the weight of her body as she moved with him.

"Dan?"

"Alice?" he mocked.

She raised her face to his. "Thanks."

"You're welcome. I make girls cry all the time. It's a special talent of mine," he said, only half joking. This time she laughed, only a little, but it was enough to make his heart trip.

"You're a dick and I still hate you."

He avoided her gaze and watched the boys turn and walk off the bridge, down the road towards them. "You can't. Your number's not up. You're only number three in line still."

"I'm a queue jumper."

Dan eased up off his arms and placed a hand on Alice's back. "Want to have a little fun?"

"Daniel!" His mother's outrage echoed through the air.

Dan chuckled. "Not that kind of fun, Mum." Although the idea was tempting. To Alice, he said, "See Slim and Lanky there? Watch this." He shifted her off his lap and got to his feet, wiping the dirt from his jeans with the palms of his hands.

Dan retrieved the carton of eggs he'd asked Maureen to bring and strolled to the corner of the building to face the newly slime-decorated side wall. Placing the box on the ground, he selected an egg, waited until the teenagers were about ten feet away then hurled an egg at a spot on the wall just above where they'd left their mark. Standing back, he admired his handiwork with a grin of smug satisfaction as the boys stopped in their tracks and stared at him.

Out the corner of his eye he caught their confusion. Lanky fiddled with his backwards cap. Slim twisted the edge of his open shirt around his fingers. Dan carefully selected another egg from the box, stepped back, toed the ground, ran up and bowled it in a spinner that would make any great cricketer proud. He dusted off his hands, watching the shell shatter, mix with the splash of yolk and egg white, catch the stream and slide gracefully into the congealed mess of its predecessors.

"Hi John...Tim." Dan bent to pick up another egg from the box. A beamer should do it this time— fast and hard. The egg hit the wall with a satisfying smack, splattering shell and goo in an impressive arch.

"Fucking oath!" muttered Tim, the lanky one.

"Language, guys. We have ladies present." He held out an egg. "Wanna have a go?"

John held up his hands and backed away. "No f —friggin' way."

Dan shrugged. "Tim?"

"Man, I don't get it. You're egging your own wall?"

"I figured I might as well finish what you boys started. You know...have a little fun so at least cleaning it is worth my time."

"You're crazy."

Dan wiggled the egg in the distance between them. "Take it and make it a good one."

Reluctantly, Tim took the egg and tossed it in a half-hearted, self-conscious effort. The egg cracked with a pathetic splat and the contents dribbled half-heartedly as it fell heavily to the ground. Curly squawked and flew in to peck at the remains.

"Need some work on that elbow action there, Tim. Next time you boys swing by, bring a tennis ball and I'll show you how to bowl." He looked at John. "Sure you don't want to have a go?" At the shake of the boy's head, Dan shrugged. "Okay then. I don't suppose either of you are any good with those spray cans in your pockets? You know...as in actual graffiti rather than tags and foul language?"

Alice watched Dan toss eggs at the wall and talk to the boys, shaking her head in disbelief. She felt

Maureen's arm slip around her shoulders and pull her into a hug.

"You okay, love?"

"Yes, thanks. Your son is something else."

Maureen laughed. "This is the most relaxed I've seen him in a long while. He's had a rough time of it. I think Charlie and Jake are great company for him."

"They do seem to be getting along well, don't they?"

She studied Dan carefully. He'd discarded his tear-damp shirt for the egg tossing and the black T-shirt he'd worn under it hugged his muscular frame like an old lover, confident in its right to be there. For a city boy, he was built. It looked like he'd made good use of his gym membership. Either that or his briefcase was damn heavy.

His jeans hung low on his hips, his stance careless and relaxed. She blushed and looked away before she could contemplate what lay below the buckle of his leather belt.

"Like you, he's been hurt, Alice, and it almost destroyed his soul. If Edwina Lette were to bring out her voodoo and define him, she'd say his soul urge number was a six. He's a man with a deep inner desire for a stable, loving family or community, a need to work with others and to be appreciated."

Alice looked at her hands—workers hands—strong, flawed with scars from run-ins with rescue animals. No salon nails for her, she decided. The maintenance was too high and she liked getting her hands dirty. Not the type of woman a city boy would even look at. "Maybe we should enter him in Bindarra Creek's Hottest Bachelor competition, or he could go online dating on the days our internet connection is actually working. I'm sure he'll find a suitable wife."

Maureen smiled and put an affectionate arm through Alice's. "Oh, love, I'm not trying to sell him to you!" She moved to stand in front of Alice, effectively blocking her view. "Men think women are hard to understand, but let me tell you, they're wrong. My son is a complicated sonofabitch and he was a terror throughout his teenage years. He didn't get that arm for egg tossing from me. He grew it all on his own as he went from phase to phase trying to find himself."

"Maureen, I—"

Dan's mum cupped a hand to her face. "I'm babbling, I know. There's a reason he hauled you out of the ute, love. He feels your pain in facing the past and dealing with it. He's passionate, compassionate, intuitive, romantic, humanitarian, broadminded and generous."

"You're selling him again."

"Did I mention romantic?" Maureen teased. "I'm his mum and I'm proud of it, proud of the man he's become despite—and because of—what he's been through. Because he's so affectionate and giving, he's also easily imposed upon and taken advantage of."

"And that's because his expression number is a nine," said Edwina Lette, her voice smokey from years of lighting up her 'medicinal' rollies.

"Good God, Edwina!" Maureen slammed a hand to her chest. "I swear the rumours are true and you really are a witch. Must you sneak up on people like that?"

Edwina sniffed. "You hear the best conversations when no-one's looking. Hi, Alice."

"Ms Lette, how are you today?"

"I'd be better if you hadn't told Dodge about my hydroponic set-up in the shed. He'll do anything to get me to quit, but it's my choice and I'll only give up when I'm good and ready."

"Edwina!" Maureen slapped her left hand up to cover the right one over her heart.

"What? It's medicinal."

Alice grinned. She adored Edwina, Bindarra

Creek's self-proclaimed psychic and tarot reader. Former town constable Dodge's wise grandmother saw too much, even without the help of her cards. "Now, Ms Lette, you know I can't let you get away with more than the one plant the government allows."

"You're right, of course, dear. It's just too damned inconvenient to have to go out into the garden at night. So what do we have here then?" She waved across to where Dan looked as if he was describing something to the two boys whose attention he commanded.

"Discipline 101 Molyneaux-style," explained Maureen.

"Good looking boy you have there, Maureen. Makes me wish I was a few years younger. Came to have a sticky beak. He has a good aura, a healthy green." Her glance slid to Alice. "A good match for a tan one."

Alice rolled her eyes. "I hope you find him a good match then."

"Good matches, my dear Alice, find each other as long as the shadows let them. Let the rainbows in, girl, you deserve it. Self-inflicted penance shouldn't last forever." Edwina fiddled in her pocket. "Damn it! Speaking of matches, I left my smokes at home.

Pam's been watching me like a bloody hawk since I said I was giving up. Can't even sneak one past her." With one last look at Dan and a satisfied-sounding hum, she turned and walked away.

"She freaks me out when she does that," said Maureen, sinking into a chair.

Alice grinned. "Me too, but she's a sweetheart and she means well."

She studied Dan thoughtfully in the group where Charlie and Jake had joined discussions with the two boys. A little over a week ago Edwina had said she'd meet someone who'd change her life by accident. In the space of thirty six hours, Dan had forced her to face her fears and physically hauled her out of her comfort zone. She waited for the rush of anxiety, the dark fear that usually gripped her whenever she came within spitting distance of the pub. All she felt was the zing of awareness that took hold of her body as Dan caught her looking and winked.

CHAPTER SIX

A week later, Dan stood in his kitchen at the back of the pub and admired the shine of the stainless steel prep tables and industrial baking oven. The old cooker hood, now thankfully cockroach-free, was scrubbed and polished to perfection. White tiles gleamed beneath his feet, the grouting between them sealed against residue oils, fats and cooking stains.

Gone was the seventies burnt orange linoleum-lined floor, the old clunky fridge had been replaced with a double-door, glass-fronted one that would soon display fresh fruit and veg, and ingredients for the tasty pub menu Maureen had planned.

Upstairs, things remained unchanged. He'd still not made it past the bottom three stairs—not without

Alice. Upstairs was personal, and even though he'd begun to see the ice slowly melt around her heart, he'd still not been able to get her through the doors of the pub.

On the upside though, his plans to open by Christmas were well under way and Muttley had taken his first steps outside the pouch this morning.

Dan dialled Alice's number as he strolled into the bar area with Muttley hopping contentedly behind him. The morning sun warmed the floor through the east-side windows, spotlighting the changes he, Charlie and Jake had made. The jarrah tables had been sanded back and the scars treated with orange oil.

Gone was the rickety old bar counter, a remnant of the eighties and nothing more than two long shelves wacked together with a couple of stays and rusty nails. As he waited for Alice to answer, he wondered why her husband hadn't modernised the pub himself.

"Hi, Dan."

"That's a big step, Alice. I'm not sure I'm ready for that kind of commitment." He tried to keep the grin off his face and failed. Talking to her, teasing her —it all came so easily.

"What are you on about?"

"You knew it was me." He heard her sigh and leaned back against the wooden post that would soon support his new bar counter.

"Yes, your name's listed in my phone twice— once under B for Bastard and then under D for Dickhead."

"Still haven't forgiven me, have you?"

"You manhandled me out of my ute, dropped me in the dirt and made me ugly cry. What do you think?"

Dan hugged the phone closer and watched Muttley clean himself in the sunny spot he'd found to lie in. The memory of holding Alice in his arms flooded him with warmth.

She'd filled them so nicely, felt so perfect, so right there. If they'd not had an audience that day, he would have pressed a kiss to her forehead and promised her he'd fix her pain.

"Dan?"

He shook off the vision of Alice in his arms and what a simple kiss could lead to. "Muttley's out of the pouch and walking around. I took him out back into the long grass and he poked around there for a bit."

"That's great news. Another couple of months and I can reintroduce him to the wild."

Dan pushed off the post and walked through the front door out onto the veranda. The early morning breeze settled around him, cool and brisk. "Yeah."

"You've grown attached to him."

"It's kinda hard not to."

"I warned you about that."

"Yes, you did. I met Maki and his donkey yesterday. They walked by while Muttley and I were out exploring the old beer garden." He heard her sharp intake of breath at the mention of the garden.

"That's nice." Her voice strained as she bit out the words.

Interesting, thought Dan. Did every corner of the pub hold bad memories for Alice? Did she have any good ones at all? "Muttley and Tails had a good time. Best of friends by the time they left."

"A play date, how sweet. Soon they'll be playing dress-ups and inviting you to a tea party."

Dan chuckled. "As long as they don't make me wear a dress." Alice's laugh tickled his senses and filled his heart with warmth. "You should laugh more often. It suits you."

"Dan—" the warning in her tone unmistakeable. *Back off, don't get too personal.*

"Alice." He watched the group of CWA ladies walking towards the pub, determination in their step.

"Bring Muttley over this afternoon and I'll introduce him to a mob I have up here. They're due for release soon. It'll be a good exercise for him."

"I'll do that. Looks like I'm about to be bailed up by the CWA. They're looking very official today."

"Good luck. There's no stopping them when they're on a mission."

Dan snorted. "Yeah, thanks. Hey, Alice?"

"Yeah?"

"See you later." Dan couldn't resist injecting an intimate tone into the words, satisfied when he heard Alice's growl a second before she hung up. He leaned against the railings as he watched the CWA approach. They'd brought the big guns. Pamela Brown led the troops, her formidable expression set, her stride determined.

"Daniel, good morning. We'd like to talk to you about hosting the Bushman's Ball this year. It's an annual fundraising event and your shed is perfect for it."

With a sigh, Dan greeted the ladies, realising this wasn't a request but more of a command, and whether or not he wanted to, he'd be hosting a ball as part of his opening celebrations.

The morning slipped by as Alice did her rounds and chores. She tried to tell herself that the expectation she felt wasn't excitement, that seeing Dan again didn't matter—especially on her own turf. She sighed as she tossed the vegetable scraps into the chicken pen.

But, damn him, she'd caught herself smiling whenever her phone rang and his name came up on the screen. Then he'd go and use that tone. The one that made her heart skip a beat and her tummy do somersaults. Dan Molyneaux didn't play fair.

Charlie, the old devil, didn't help either with his constant reminders of how he spent his time down at the pub with Jake. Not that she minded him helping out down there. It gave him something to do and from the sound of things, Dan was taking great care with the restorations. Pete hadn't been interested— not in restoring the pub or the gym her grandfather had once taught boxing in. All he'd seen was a way out through the insane offers developers were making on properties in dying Bindarra Creek.

He'd never really wanted the responsibility of running the family pub. No, he'd wanted to head west to the mining boom and the lure of big money and iron ore. The new gold, he'd called it. That's where his dreams had lain and he'd been itching to shake Bindarra Creek's dust from his boots.

Alice had argued. She loved the town, its history and the people. Even when other young families were heading to the city or west to the mines, she'd had no desire to leave. She'd been so excited when she'd found out she was pregnant, so sure Pete would change his mind and settle down to raise a family in the small community she loved so much. Instead, things between them deteriorated. They'd argued constantly in those last days, their marriage in tatters as their dreams tore them in opposite directions. And then that awful night.

"Alice!" Dan waved as he crossed the bridge, Muttley following close behind with Curly riding the roo's shoulder.

"Alice, Alice," squawked the parrot.

Alice dusted off her hands on her jeans and watched the joey hop from side to side before peering through the rail into the river. Braced by his tail, he stretched and twitched his ears, catching new sounds from the banks. Muttley, bless him, still had to grow into his legs but it wouldn't be long before he was ready to join a mob in the wild. Dan called to him, a squeaking noise Curly imitated and they stepped off the bridge onto the gravel path leading to the sanctuary.

"Careful there, City Boy, the bush is rubbing off on you." She nodded towards his red and grey flannel shirt flapping in the breeze over a black T-shirt. He'd ripped the sleeves out of the flanno, exposing nicely toned arms Alice could quite happily watch at work lifting and carrying anything. His jeans fit well, hugging all the right places and a few she'd prefer not to be drawn to.

And there it was—that grin that teased at her sense of humour and dared her to grin back. Muttley studied her hesitantly. Avoiding Dan's gaze, she knelt to the joey's level and called to him, a piece of wattle bark from her feed bucket stretched towards him. He inched forward and took a nibble. Alice let go and the joey settled at her feet to chew the bark.

"You have a way with animals."

She felt Dan's gaze on her head, but concentrated on Muttley. "I guess I do." Inching her way forward, she lay on the grassy patch next to the joey, mimicking the way a kangaroo doe would relax, and carried out a subtle scrutiny of his condition. She had to hand it to Dan, Muttley looked great.

Satisfied, she ignored the hand Dan extended and stood without his help. Somehow she misjudged and came up a whole lot closer than intended, her body brushing his. Or maybe he moved, because his arm came around her waist to steady her as she stumbled back, and she found herself fitted to the hard curves of his torso. Her hands connected with his chest, intent on pushing him away. Instead her palm stuck like a fly on a white shirt.

Under her palms, his muscles flexed and his chest expanded on a sharply indrawn breath. For a fleeting moment, she caught his gaze—intense, fiery, alive—and felt the ground shift beneath her with the stirring of attraction. Her fingers curled, gripping his T-shirt in a fist. The hand not securing her waist enfolded her fist in his palm, warm and solid.

"Alice?" His breath whispered across her forehead, teased the strands of hair that had broken free from the tight ponytail she'd bound them in.

She closed her eyes to the tenderness in his tone, clenched her thighs against the desire sent spiralling through her by the play of his thumb on her spine, and willed her feet to move out of the space he'd commandeered.

"Let's introduce Muttley to the mob." As his arms slowly fell away to release her, she opened her eyes and stepped away.

Dan shoved his hands into the pockets of his

jeans, lifted his shoulders and released a long breath. "Of course."

"How's his diet?" Alice ignored the indications of how their close contact had affected Dan. No good could come from hooking up with a city boy, even if she was attracted for the first time in years. She swept up the feed bucket and strode purposefully towards the kangaroo enclosure with Muttley following the trail of lucerne chaff that fell with each swing of her arm.

"Well—other than the odd beer and bowl of cereal—he likes grass."

"Beer?" Surely he wasn't serious? Alice turned to find him right behind her. "You're kidding right?"

Dan shrugged. "Maybe. Okay, yes. He's drinking less milk and eating more grass. He likes muesli—"

"Muesli, that's good."

"With his beer."

"Dan!"

"Alice."

"You're impossible." Alice's lips twitched. "Please tell me he doesn't really drink beer?" His eyes twinkled with laughter and Alice punched his arm.

"Ouch."

"Serves you right," she muttered. "How did you

go with the ladies from the CWA this morning?" The smile on his lips faded along with the light in his eyes. Alice's stomach churned.

"We need to talk."

"About what?" Dread stole her breath as his jaw clenched.

"About upstairs."

Shadows crept in and seized her mind, paralysing her muscles. Her throat closed around her protest as she swayed against the blackness swimming in her vision. Alice squeezed her eyes shut to stop the monster of anxiety from stealing her sanity. She felt his strong hands reach for her shoulders and steady her, but unlike before, Dan didn't draw her close. Instead, he held her at arm's length.

"Look at me, Alice," he demanded.

She let her eyes flutter open and focus on his eyes—the deep green irises, the sweep of lashes edged with gold and the laughter lines that fanned from the corners.

"That's my girl. Breathe with me."

She slowed her breathing to match the rhythm of his and felt the black wave recede with each exhale. When her heart rate settled, she relaxed her shoulders but he didn't drop his hands.

Disappointment replaced the fear when he didn't pull her into his arms and hold her against his heartbeat. She longed to hear it echoed with her own, to feel secure again, to feel loved. Only when her breathing returned to normal did he relax his hold on her long enough to tip up her chin with his finger.

"You okay?"

Alice nodded. The tightness in her throat and sting behind her eyelids reminded her that if she spoke now, there'd be no holding back the tears. She'd avoided it for too long, and now the moment she'd been dreading had arrived. Had she really thought she could ignore it forever?

Dan released his hold on her chin and took her hand instead. In the far corner of the enclosure a wooden rest bench stood in the shade of a gum tree. He led her to it, sat down and tugged on her hand until she sat next to him. Shoulders touching, he kept hold of her hand. She should protest, pull away, but his touch was firm and reassuring as he entwined his fingers with hers.

"The CWA want me to host the Bushman's Ball in December. They tell me my shed used to be a popular venue back in the day."

Alice wiped away a stray tear with her free hand.

"Yes, Charlie owned the pub back then, way before I was born. I don't think Bindarra Creek has hosted the ball in over forty years."

"That's what Mrs Brown said. They want to bring it back now that the town has grown some."

"It will be good business for the pub. Good timing too, I guess."

"Their request comes with a proviso. They want people to stay over rather than drive home after the ball."

"Sounds fair. With Edwina's B&B and possibly a few rooms to rent around the place, it could work." Alice shrugged.

"I've agreed to allow some tents in the paddock at the back of the pub and the CWA will approach council for a permit to camp on the showgrounds for the weekend, maybe even set up some fair stalls."

"Great idea. What about crowd control?" She relaxed against his shoulder, the anxiety from earlier receding.

Dan grinned. "Jake's got it covered."

Alice laughed, a vision of Jake brandishing his toy gun like some big shopping centre security guard entering her mind. Dan's fingers curled around hers tightly and his mood shifted.

"They want me to apply for a temporary

accommodation license and rent out the upstairs rooms."

She squeezed his hand so tightly, he winced. Silence walked a tightrope between them as Alice fought against reality and common sense. *No!* Damn the CWA and their meddling. Why couldn't they leave the town to die? It had all started with that redevelopment grant Tessa had helped the town win. Then she'd married Dodge, worked hard at revitalising Bindarra Creek and given the town hope. Hope had turned the soil, raised new walls, and now it was tearing out her heart. She'd love to tell Dan to piss off and take his renovation plans with him, but that would be unfair on everyone in Bindarra Creek.

She drew in a deep breath, puffed out her cheeks and let it out slowly. Next to her, Dan sat silent and unmoving, a solid mass sharing her rickety bench. She found comfort in his silence. Minutes felt like hours as her mind churned over what renting out those rooms meant.

Muttley hopped up and Dan leaned over to pat his head. Curly perched on the feed bucket and helped himself to a piece of bark to nibble on. A breeze rustled the leaves of the old gum tree. Still Dan didn't utter a word. Alice chewed on her lip.

As Muttley and Curly settled in the dirt for a

play, Dan leaned back on the bench and stretched his arms out along the backrest and legs out in front of him.

"I have a small problem."

"Dan—"

"The rooms are uninhabitable."

"Throw the stuff away. I'll get a skip bin delivered."

"No."

"Yes. I can't do it. I can't go up there."

"You have to."

Alice stood and paced. "I can't."

"Charlie says you're the best man for the job."

"What?" Alice stopped mid-pace and spun around to face him.

"Your grandad reckons you're right up there with the best of them when it comes to catching possums."

Stumped, Alice stared at him. He kept his head angled towards Muttley and Curly, avoiding her gaze. "Possums?"

His lips twisted in a grin he battled to keep at bay. "Yeah, you know, those bright-eyed fluffy things that look like rats."

"Daniel!" Hands on her hips and legs apart, her use of his full name had him looking up. "I know what a friggin' possum looks like but right now, I smell a rat."

Dan tossed a gumnut for Curly to chase and helped Muttley crawl into the pouch for a rest. Her nerves stretched to breaking point as she watched him go through the motions. What was Charlie up to now? What hare-brained, half-baked scheme had the two of them cooked up?

Finally, Dan stood and dusted off his jeans. Alice waited, trying not to focus on the sweep of his hands or how the denim lovingly hugged the muscles of his thighs. Country air suited him. He'd lost the city pallor and gained a healthy bronze from the outdoors, but not even his broad shoulders taking flannel checked shirts to a whole new level of sexy would distract her from getting to the bottom of what he and her grandfather were up to.

"Well, they do smell like rats, I guess. Jake says they're nesting in the roof, and he reckons you'll know what that means." Dan strolled towards her, his long legs covering the short distance in four easy strides.

"Depends on how long they've been there and where their nest is. You could be looking at replacing all the ceilings up there. Possum pee stains them brown and the stink lingers. Not even a coat of paint will cover it up."

"That's why I need you to evict them for me."

"I'll call in the vet. He has a trap and will check them over before relocating them."

"I want you to remove them."

"I can't take on any more animals."

"They're possums, they live in little tree houses. You don't need to take them on."

"I know what you and Charlie are up to, Dan. It won't work." Alice stepped forward to poke a finger at his chest, punctuating each word as she said, "Throw. The. Stuff. Away."

Dan poked back. "No."

"Hey!" She slapped his hand away but he persisted, his fingers working their way down her side.

Dan found Alice's ticklish spot and gave it a good work over until she collapsed against him, laughing. "Aha!" Triumphantly he launched an attack on her ribs as she tried hard to push his hands away.

Helplessly, she clutched at his arms, begging him to stop between giggles. They fell down on the grass with Dan taking her weight while he continued his assault, and rolled her over so her back was on the ground. Alice's grip transferred to the open flaps of his shirt. Breathless, she cried, "Mercy!"

Dan hovered over her, supporting his weight on his arms. "I win. You're on possum patrol," he declared with a grin.

"Dan..."

This time her breath was taken from her by the mischievous glint in his eyes and the very sexy smile on his lips. The heat from his body warmed hers and stirred desire deeply buried for too long. His long legs aligned with hers and she wanted to wraps hers around them to anchor them there because, God help her, he felt like he belonged there, cradled between her hips. Her heart reached out to him. He'd made her laugh—really laugh—and that felt good too.

"Alice..."

The rise and fall of his chest against her breasts slowed to a steady breathing pattern and hers stopped altogether as his head blocked out the sun. Lifting her head, she rose to meet his lips halfway.

She wasn't even sure it was a kiss. The first touch of his lips tasted like a cocktail she'd never had before —the kind you took a sip of and then needed another so your tongue could confirm what your lips had sampled—nothing more than a mere brush of his mouth. Yet it stirred a need so deep, it clenched her stomach and made her blood sing. Not even in the rush of her youth had she felt this dizzying desire to possess and be loved in return.

Her hands let go of his shirt to creep up the strong lines of his neck and into his hair, pulling him closer. She felt the sigh of his breath against her lips the second before he took possession of her mouth and kissed her mind into oblivion. She answered him with a heat-seeking missile of her own, smiled at his intake of breath and gave back each taste and test to match.

The ice-cold spray of water slapped him between the shoulder blades and soaked through the layer of flannel and T-shirt. Dan swore he heard his skin sizzle. "What the fuck? Charlie!" Dan rolled away from Alice, hands in the air, and copped another spray in his face. "Are you crazy?" He wiped his arm across his forehead.

"I told you to convince her, not seduce her! Bloody hell, son, you've given the CWA enough gossip for the next decade. Lucky Jake loaned me his super water-blaster." He brandished the purple and green water machine gun in the air. "Looks like you two needed cooling off." Charlie chuckled as Alice covered her face with her hands, cheeks apple-red with embarrassment.

Dan stood and helped Alice to her feet. "Friggin' hell, that was cold. Did you have to use ice water?" he said to Charlie while he dusted the grass off Alice's shirt and jeans. For good measure—and because he couldn't resist it—he patted her firmly on the butt.

She planted her hands on his chest and shoved him away. "I knew you two were up to something! Is that what that was about, Dan? You think after one kiss, I'll fall at your feet and do your bidding? Well, I've got news for you, *buster*—"

She walked him backward with little pushes to his chest he could have resisted but had no desire to. Angry Alice was downright hot when she was mad. "Hey, easy," he protested when she had his back to the wooden fence around the alpaca enclosure.

She stretched on her tippy toes until her eyes were level with his. "You'll have to do better than that." Her gaze dropped to his lips, stayed there for a moment before she pushed away. "A lot better than that." She turned to walk away.

"I'm willing to give it a go if you are," he called out to her departing back. "You kissed me first!"

Charlie chuckled as Alice held her thumb and forefinger in the air in the shape of an L.

Dan wasn't laughing at all as he watched the exaggerated sway of her hips disappear over the hill and into the house. No, kissing Alice was no laughing matter at all. It left him wanting more.

CHAPTER SEVEN

*W*ith his lips still recovering from the sweet taste of Alice, his heart full of doubt and his mind awhirl, Dan wondered how the hell he would ever convince her to face her past head-on. Especially when he didn't have the balls to face his own. Sooner or later, he'd have to confront the screams that haunted his dreams and had him waking up in a sweat at night with his heart racing and guilt playing chasey in the shadows.

It wasn't until he'd crossed the bridge that he noticed what Slim and Lanky were up to. The side wall of his pub, only just having recovered from the egging, now sported an array of emoticons. Smiley faces, sad faces, smileys with sunglasses all created from the dried yellow of the egg yolks they hadn't managed to scrape off. Dan sighed. At least it was an improvement on what was there before.

"So since you guys really do suck at graffiti art, maybe you'd like to help me clean out the shed?"

"W.I.I.F.U," said Slim, finishing off a smiley slanted mouth with a slash of red.

"What?" Dan stood feet apart, hands on hips and frowned at the boys.

Lanky turned with a grin. "Relax, dude. He means what's in it for us?"

Dan snorted. "Really, because I thought he was saying something else there for a minute. Don't kids speak English anymore?"

"Nah, mate. You oldies need to get with the program. We use SMS speak," said Lanky.

"Soooo...what he said." Slim pocketed the can of spray and gave a vague tip of his head toward Lanky.

"What's in it for you? You get to hang out with this old guy, Papa Smurf, the bird you taught to swear and a joey who still needs his arse wiped occasionally. Sounds like a fair deal to me for giving my wall a facelift instead of a design." Dan turned and walked toward the shed where he pushed open the heavy old door. "Coming?"

Slim's shoulders lifted in a shrug. "Whatevs."

Lanky's eyes however lit with interest. "Holy batshit, is that a boxing bag? It must be like ancient."

Dan grinned. "Yep, somewhere around 1940 this was a boxing gym run by Alice's grandad."

"You're not going to toss it, are you?" Apparently horrified by the thought, Lanky slipped past Dan to get a better look at the boxing bag. "Oh man! This is a genuine Jack Dempsey Everlast speed bag. Check it out! It has the stamps on it and everything. This would go bananas on eBay." He sniffed the cowhide and ran his fingers over the laces. Giving the bag a squeeze, he checked the inflation valve. "Lost some air over the years but the valve is in good nick."

"Well, I'm not selling it and neither are you. How come you know about boxing bags?" said Dan.

Lanky shrugged. "My grandad was a boxer. I'd like to give it a go but he's dead now and it's not like there's a gym in Bindarra Creek."

"Mmmm...what about you, Slim?"

The boy worked hard to keep a neutral expression. He'd be no good in a poker game even when he was old enough to play. Dan had seen his eyes wander and come to a halt on the impressive weight bench.

"Not much else to do around here. I wouldn't mind a go on that." Slim nodded towards the bench.

"Okay, here's the deal. You help me clean the place up in time for the Bushman's Ball and I'll be your personal trainer. If there's enough interest, I might open a gym and look for someone to manage it."

"No way, man! You'd do that?"

"Sure. Why not? I don't see the point of good equipment going to waste." If nothing else it would help him knock out some of his own frustration, and after tasting Alice, he might need something to kick his addiction to her lips. God help him, one kiss was not going to be enough. And if she thought he needed practice, he'd sure as hell show her what he was capable of. She'd thrown down the gauntlet and he was happy to pick it up.

"Not a word, Charlie! Not one bloody smart-arsed comment, okay?"

Walking back up from the house where she'd splashed cold water on her burning cheeks, Alice picked up the bucket she'd dropped while rolling around on the grass with Dan. The man should come with a hazard warning. She could still feel the imprint of his hand on her backside and the touch of his lips on hers. And oh my God, when his hands had roamed her body in a show of dusting her off...

She almost regretted the taunt she'd delivered with his back up against the fence. If Dan Molyneaux had tried any harder, not even a blast of cold water would have stopped her from ravaging him right there in full view of anyone who might have walked past. Her cheeks grew warm again at the thought of what might have happened if Charlie hadn't shown up when he did.

"My lips are sealed. I can't speak for the CWA ladies who were on their way over to ask if you'd man a stall at the Sunday markets this weekend." Charlie winked.

"Oh my God, Pop!" Alice squeezed her eyes shut. The grapevine would run hot over high tea this afternoon. "Please tell me they were too far away to see what was going on?"

"I think I even saw Edwina take a snapshot. She'll sell it to the local newspaper for a story. Imagine the headlines."

"Pop, no!"

Charlie grinned. "I'm kidding, love." He put an arm around her shoulders and hugged her hard, giving her a little shake while he was at it. "So you kissed the guy, that's not a bad thing is it?"

"He kissed me first!"

"And from what I saw, you kissed him right back. Good on ya! He's a good bloke."

Alice studied the rusty roof of the pub, her thoughts coming back to what lay just beneath it. "Will you come with me, Pop?"

"I'll be there with you when you're ready. It's time, Alice."

"No, it's way past time but I'm still not sure I can make myself go up those stairs."

"Then we'll do it together."

"I love you, Pop." She kissed his leathery cheek. He smelled like hard work and old age...like home.

"I love you too." With one last squeeze he let go of her shoulders and hobbled towards the alpacas. "Oh, and Al...?" he called over his shoulder. "Edwina has ten bucks on a marriage proposal by Christmas."

Alice groaned.

CHAPTER EIGHT

*T*he morning sun crept in through valley mist and cast a beam on the side wall of the pub. Dan grinned widely. So the little hell-raisers really could draw after all. He could see their renewed attempts to remove the remains of the egg, and in the corner closest to the shed was a caricature of a boxing ring with two tall and lanky teenagers sparring. On the ropes sat Curly, while Muttley watched from below. Above it, in graffiti writing of course—had he expected anything less?—a sign declared it the BCG.

Yes! Dan fist-pumped the air. Finally, a breakthrough and he couldn't be prouder if he'd fathered the kids himself. He picked up the hoe and began clearing the weeds from what used to be the floor of the beer garden. Maybe he'd make a better publican than an investment broker after all.

Here in this small but growing town, he could make a difference. He could help people change their lives for the better, and none of it involved money or selling the benefits of an investment.

"Morning," greeted Jake, hitching up the legs of his worn corduroys as he waded through the waist-length grass towards him. "Might have to take a bloody old-fashioned sickle to this shit before we mow it. That old push mower in the shed won't cut it."

Dan smiled cunningly. "You underestimate the power of my charm. One of the ladies at the CWA has arranged a ride-on mower through the station owner at Bindarra Downs. He'll bring it over later. We'll knock it over in a day. Gotta love the country. If we were in Sydney, I'd have to fork out a fortune for a lawn mowing service."

"Ah, yes, young Cameron Reid. Good bloke that. Is there anything that cheeky grin of yours can't buy?" Jake snorted. "I'll be in the shed if you need me."

"Sure, cheers Jake." Dan's grin turned to a grimace. His cheeky grin couldn't buy him peace of mind and a good night's sleep. The recurring nightmares hadn't faded, but on the upside, Alice's appearance in his dreams close to dawn had eased the fear. His heart had beat out a different rhythm then and he was still smiling at his reflection later when he'd brushed his teeth and shaved the night's growth from his chin.

Would she come by today after what happened between them? Had he blown the foundations of a friendship to hell? But no, she had kissed him back, that had to count for something. Maybe he was crazy wanting a relationship with Alice in any form. She didn't need another fucked-up individual in her life. Not after what happened to her family, especially not a man who had destroyed someone else's life.

But there was something about Alice that struck a chord deep inside his heart, a place no other woman had yet to reach. He found himself drawn closer every time he saw her, bantered with her, kissed her.

Shrugging off his shirt and tossing it aside, Dan grabbed the rake from against the wall and dragged the loosened weeds into a neat pile. Maybe somewhere under years of sand and weeds, he'd find the concrete floor he was sure would still be there. Now if only he could rake up his own shit and find his own foundations again, life would be sweet. Dan the cheerful larrikin was a hard mask to maintain every day when inside guilt ate away at his happiness.

Strangely enough, Bindarra Creek had proved cathartic physically and perhaps for the first time he could remember, he felt at home. It was the screams that haunted his dreams that held him back. No matter what kind of a bastard Harris was, he didn't deserve to die the way he did. No-one deserved that.

The brown stain on the pavement that had taken the council weeks to clean away, the commuters on busy Bridge Street stepping around it, the floral tributes to the man who'd died there, irrespective of his reputation in the business world—the visions had burned themselves into every recess of his memory so that every time he closed his eyes, he saw it, heard it, felt the wrench of horror and helplessness in his gut, and smelled the coppery tang of blood.

Dropping the rake, he clamped his hands over his ears as even now the screams pierced his eardrums.

Well, God damn him for standing there all shirtless and sexy with his jeans hanging low on his hips and his city muscles bared to the cool morning. Alice hoped he'd catch a cold. It would serve him right for haunting her thoughts all night long as she'd tried to figure him out. Looked like a god, kissed like a demon and behaved like an angel of mercy when needed. Men like him didn't exist unless they had a Y-chromosome anomaly and made better friends than boyfriends.

She'd walked to the pub this morning with the hope of driving him from her thoughts so she could focus on the task that lay ahead. Cleansing—finally facing the chore she'd put off for so long. How did one purge happy memories even when they were laced with sadness and the mistakes of youth?

Seeing Dan drop the rake and clamp his hands over his ears, her heart skipped a beat. She watched as his shoulders hunched and tensed, the muscles in his back becoming rigid. Something was bugging the city boy and it didn't look good on him.

Alice stepped up and placed a firm slap between his shoulder blades then let her hand linger a little longer. The skin was warm beneath her palm. He smelled like man, soap, sweat and earth so she breathed him in. "Swallow a fly, Greenie? You should learn to keep your mouth closed."

His muscles jumped under her palm as he

dropped his arms and his gaze. She caught a quick glimpse of torment in his eyes before he looked over her head and stepped away. She allowed her hand to stay outstretched for a moment before dropping it to her hip. Touching him was becoming too easy, too familiar.

He picked up the rake and balanced it against the wall, the silence thick in the misty morning air. Alice shivered. Where had Dan gone that had made him so tense and sad? Pushing down the lick of disappointment, she watched as he shrugged back into his shirt.

"You okay, Dan?"

He nodded, rolled his shoulders and rubbed the back of his neck. "Yeah."

"Liar."

He shrugged. Where was the banter, the comeback, the twinkle in his eye? She missed it and wanted it back because this was a side of Dan she couldn't deal with, not today when she'd made up her mind to exorcise her own demons—not any day.

"Want to talk about it?"

"No."

Alice sighed. She was so not good at this anymore. With Pete, she'd ignored his sulks knowing he'd get over it in his own time, but Dan was different. Whatever plagued him was etched into the tight pull of his jaw and the hardness of his lips.

"You mad at me?"

"No."

"Have Slim and Lanky annoyed you?"

"No."

"Something happened to Muttley?"

"For God's sake, Alice, no!" he roared. With a sweep of his hand, the hoe and the rake clattered to the ground. His flashing gaze found hers, hot and angry.

Alice stood, feet apart, and stared him down. If Dan thought he could scare her off, he could think again. She'd been awake all night mulling over things, steeling herself against the pain the task ahead would bring. And if she could do it, damn it, so could he.

"Well, something's crawled up your arse."

Dan looked away, raked a hand through his hair and sighed. "Sorry, you caught me at a bad moment." He picked up the toppled tools. "Hi, Alice."

"Hi, Dan." She grinned. When he grinned back, albeit half-heartedly, her heart did that little flip-flop thing. "So are you going to tell me what you're mad about?"

"No."

Alice sighed. "Fine, suit yourself." She turned on her heel and began to walk away with small, slow, deliberate steps. "You can tell the CWA I came over to clear the upstairs rooms and sort out your possum problem, but you were too busy being a bad-tempered grump to play."

"Wait! *What?*"

She waved a hand over head. "Nope, see you later. You're on your own. Pamela Brown will have a field day over your lack of co-operation. And then there's the matter of the expense involved when the ceiling comes crashing down, possums and all."

"Alice!"

"Alice, Alice," called Curly, swooping down to walk next to her in a drunken swagger. "You okay, mate?"

"Hey, Curly. Who taught you that? At least your vocabulary is improving."

"Fuck."

"Okay, maybe not." She lifted her face to the sky as the sun broke through a misty patch, then squealed as strong hands encircled her waist and spun her around.

Her nose brushed against Dan's chest before he held her away at arm's length. "What did you say?"

"I said Curly is on his way to being almost human with his vocabulary."

This time his smile reached his eyes and it made her heart pound. "You idiot." He cupped her cheek with his palm and stroked his thumb across her skin. "What did you say before that?"

"I came over to clean out the rooms upstairs." Her breath hitched and she cursed herself for her weakness, and for adding his pain to hers.

Dan pulled her into his arms and held on tight. "I'm a bastard. I'm sorry."

"Yes," replied Alice, her face still buried against him, her lips moving against the warm skin of his chest. "You are." And because she kinda liked the taste of his skin on her lips, she continued, "I'll never forgive you, of course." Maybe she should just keep talking. She stifled the sweep of disappointment when his finger raised her chin and swept her lips away from the warmth so her eyes could see the seriousness in his.

"That's a big decision."

"Yes."

"Wow."

"Really wow." Alice lifted a hand to touch his cheek. "Where did you go just then?"

Dan sighed. "To a horrible place I never want to

go back to. I'm sorry. Every now and then, the memories catch me off guard."

"I remember some dumb-arse city boy telling me not so long ago about how he'd bought this pub and couldn't get it up and running with my ghosts still in residence? He made me stare my anxiety monsters in the face, forced me out of my comfort zone and annoyed the crap out of me by phoning me at ungodly hours to talk shit. Maybe it's time that guy faced his own ghosts."

Dan leaned his forehead against hers. "Maybe."

"Let me help you, Molyneaux."

"It's a long story."

"You've got five minutes. Make it happen."

He chuckled and the sexiness of it made her shiver. She cuddled closer. No time for distance now, not when they both needed strength. Dan had held her through two anxiety attacks, she could return the favour, right? Alice wrapped her arms around his waist and let her head rest on his chest. His breath shuddered in and out under her ear. She closed her eyes to listen to the rhythm and waited patiently for him to gather his thoughts.

"Six months ago I had a client on my books. He lost big money—all of it—and he blamed me. He sank a small fortune into a Western Australian quayside apartment development portfolio I'd recommended. Not long into development, the construction site was damaged in a storm off the coast. Insurance wouldn't pay out because it was a natural disaster and the builder only had insurance on workmanship and engineering. Everyone lost money, but Harris took it the worst because he owned the largest share. He committed suicide from the top of my office building. Fell right past my window. He had a family—a wife and two daughters. I did what I could to help, but it will never be enough. It will never bring him back." Dan's hands left her waist as he sunk them into his hair, dragging it back.

"Oh Jesus, Dan!" Alice swallowed hard against the horror of the picture he drew in her mind.

"Everyone reassured me it wasn't my fault. He was in debt up to his eyeballs long before that development crashed. Every time he made money, he pissed it into the wind, gambled and sometimes won then he'd sink it into another poor investment. I knew that and still I did nothing to discourage him. I might as well have pushed him off that roof myself."

"That's bullcrap and you know it!" Alice slapped a hand to his chest. "He made the choice to jump, he made the decisions to sign up for that investment. We can't control the decisions people make, Dan."

"My mind tells me you're right, but it's hard to get that picture out of my head. The investigations went on for months, my name was dragged through the mud and my reputation questioned. You know how the media works. It's not a story unless they bend the truth. The reputation of the company my mother started and built from the ground up crumbled. I failed her, I failed myself."

"You did not fail her! Your mother is proud of you. Good Lord, when she found out you were coming to town, the whole of Bindarra Creek knew the Great Daniel Molyneaux was on his way. You might have made an error of judgment, or maybe you didn't. Let me ask you this: if you'd advised Harris against investing in that project, would he have listened to you?"

Dan shrugged. "Probably not? All he saw was the money it could make and it was my job to sell him the long term benefits."

Alice shuddered. All Pete had seen was the money too. "If it wasn't for the storm, would it have been a successful long term investment?"

"Yes."

"You would have done the research before you signed anyone up for that project. I don't believe you would have knowingly put anyone at risk, financially or otherwise. A guy who can name a bloody orphaned joey wouldn't put a man's life on the line." She touched his cheek gently, worked her hands around the back of his neck and pulled his face in line with hers. "Let it go, Dan. What happened is not your fault. We all make decisions in life that turn out either good or bad. That's how we learn to move forward." Stretching up on her toes, she kissed him hard and fast on the lips. "The bad dreams will go away eventually, trust me. Life always has a plan for us. That's what Charlie keeps telling me and I want to believe him."

"I'd like to believe that too. But I keep thinking, wondering what if I'd discouraged him knowing what I knew—"

"The storm would still have happened, just in another form. It sounds like he was a man on a path to destruction. I recognise that. Pete was headed the same way. I just couldn't acknowledge it then, and I had no power to stop it."

"I'm sorry."

"Stop saying that. There are things in life we can change and then there are the things we can't." Drawing his gaze to hers, she held it a moment, absorbing his pain and anger, letting it mingle with hers. "We both need to let go, Dan. Maybe if we do it together, the pain won't be so bad. Let's go exorcise a few ghosts, shall we?"

Dan drew her against him and kissed her softly. "You're one hell of a woman, Alice."

"I'm glad you think so," she whispered, her lips moving against his, the taste addictive yet soothing. "You're not bad either...for a city boy."

His lips took possession of hers and for one blissful moment, all thoughts of ghosts fled. Alice relaxed against him, absorbing his warmth and the feel of his skin beneath her hands. The play of his fingers on her spine combined with the hardening of his body against hers sent delicious shivers through her. Oh God, he made her feel loved and wanted and *alive* again. Happiness spiralled through her, warming her heart and mind. Some unknown power of fate had brought them together and it would be a shame to waste that opportunity.

She kissed him back, opening her mouth to the exploration of his tongue, let her hands wander to the hips she'd admired earlier and around to...oh yes, a *very* feel-worthy arse. His muscles tightened under her touch and for a second, Alice wished they were naked so she could appreciate the feel of those muscles without the barrier of clothing.

"Alice," he whispered, withdrawing his mouth from hers to trail kisses down her neck.

She arched into him as he bent and drew her hips up to meet his. Dizzying need had her pressing closer and she closed her eyes to imagine what it would be like being intimate with Dan. His touch was gentle, creating a slow burn that had her melting like candle wax. There'd be no hard and fast loving from Dan Molyneaux, at least not today.

He lifted her into his arms and she wrapped her legs around him, burying her face in the warmth of his neck as he pressed a tender kiss to her temple. He cradled her close as the tension left his body. Alice lifted her face to his and smiled. For a long moment, their gazes held, forging a bond of understanding, acceptance and inner peace.

"Thank you," he said.

"For what?"

"For being you."

"That's the easy part—the 'me' I am now. It's the 'me' I was who needs cleansing, Dan. I'm going to need help with that."

"Looks like we're in this together."

"I like the sound of that." Alice cupped his cheeks and pressed her lips to his. "I like it a lot." The rumble of a diesel engine approaching had her casting a look over Dan's shoulder. "You'll have to put me down. Grandad Charlie's coming."

"His timing really sucks." Dan sighed as he let Alice slide down his body and anchored her hand in his. "I'll have to talk to him about that. On the upside, it looks like he's brought Cameron Reid and the ride-on mower with him, so I'll have to let it slide this time."

Alice chuckled. "You're a cheap mark, Dan Molyneaux, easily bought for a piece of machinery. I don't know if I can associate with a man like that."

He squeezed her fingers lightly before letting go of her hand. "Oh, we're not done yet, Alice." His gaze smouldered with promise.

"Not by a mile, GQ." Her heart squeezed with an emotion she wasn't ready to name. "I'll go check on Muttley while you play with your big boy's toys."

"He's in the shed with Jake. You okay with that?"

Concern flashed in his eyes and Alice felt her heart tumble inside her chest. If she wasn't careful she'd be head over heels in love with this city-boy-turned-publican in a flash. She reached up to kiss his cheek. "The shed I can handle. It's only Charlie's memories in there."

Dan watched Alice turn and walk away toward the shed, his hands fisted in the pockets of his jeans and his cheek warm from her kiss. Hell, who was he kidding? His whole friggin' body was on fire for Alice, but had they gone too far too quickly? God, he hoped not. The spark between them ran deeper than mere attraction and he wasn't one hundred percent sure that was a good thing. It felt good. Christ, it felt good, but if it didn't work out between them—he shook off his doubts as the diesel truck towing a trailer pulled up outside the pub.

Charlie hopped out the passenger side. "Did I just see you with your hands on my granddaughter again?"

"Er, Charlie?" Dan scraped his thumb across his brow, feeling like a schoolboy caught necking on the sofa.

"Not that I'm objecting or anything, but you do know there's money on it down at the CWA, right?"

Dan rolled his eyes. "How much have you got down, Charlie?"

The old man chuckled. "Wouldn't you love to know?" His eyes watered. "You go easy on my girl, okay? Otherwise you'll have a lynch mob on your tail and nothing will save you from their wrath."

Dan nodded. "I get that."

"Good. This here is Cam from Bindarra Downs."

The young station owner held out a friendly hand and Dan shook it firmly. "Hey, Cam. Thanks for the loan of the mower."

Cam shrugged. "That's what we do around here. I look forward to the old place reopening and seeing what you've done with it. I'll off-load now and pick it up again tomorrow? Will that give you enough time?"

"Plenty, thanks. I appreciate it, man."

"So I hear you're hosting the Bushman's Ball this year?"

"Seems that way. I wasn't planning to but no-one says no to the ladies at the CWA, I'm told."

Cam grinned. "I know I'm not game to. If you need help, yell out."

"I might take you up on that offer. Not sure I'd know the first thing about setting it up." Dan scratched his head.

"Ask Alice to arrange a committee to help with the planning." Cam winked. "From the looks of things, you two are getting cosy. I'm sure she'd help out."

Dan blew out a breath. "Please don't tell me you have money down at the CWA too?"

"Mate, everyone has money down since you

came to town. Proceeds go to the next big town project if you come through."

"Nothing like small town community pressure. Maybe I should set you all straight so you can put your money to good use. Alice and I understand each other. Neither of us is ready for a relationship. We're friends, that's all." Dan tried hard to keep the defensiveness from his tone, but failed.

"Easy, man. The community means well. It's not about the bets or the next project. They care about Alice, and about you too. She deserves a chance at happiness and if you're the bloke to give her that, we're all behind you. Speaking of happiness, I better unload the mower and head back to Bindarra Downs or I'll be sleeping in the shed tonight. Come on over and meet Rhiannon sometime. She's a city girl. You can bring her up to speed on what's going on outside our little town."

"Sounds good, thanks Cam." He walked beside the young station owner to the trailer.

They unbolted the tailgate and lowered the ramp before Cam hopped up to ride the mower down. Minutes later Dan waved Cam goodbye and drove the machine towards the paddock behind the pub. His mind churned over the town's expectations of a relationship between him and Alice. What if it didn't work out between them? He was crazy to even think of hooking up with her. If it fell apart, one of them would have to leave town. He didn't want it to be him. Not when he'd finally come home. But he wouldn't be able to stay knowing he'd hurt her after all she'd been through. No, the best thing he could do for them both was to stay the hell away.

Row after row Dan rode the machine, the smell of freshly mowed weeds in his nose and Alice on his mind. He made the turn at the end of the paddock and looked across at the shed. There she was, playing with Muttley, her laughter ringing out over the creek, her face turned upwards to the sky. Who was he kidding? He was on the downhill slide to falling hopelessly in love.

"Are you going to sit up there like a lovesick lothario or are you going to get that girl to sort out your possum problem before we have a marsupial population explosion?"

Sprung, Dan looked down to meet the amusement in Jake's eyes. "You know how to sneak up on a man."

"I made so much damn noise wading through this grass I could've woken the whole bloody jungle. You were so wrapped up I'm surprised you mowed a straight line. Get off and leave it to the expert, son. Alice needs you."

Dan swung his leg over and hopped off the mower. "All yours, old man." He brushed residue grass from his denim-clad thighs, leaving green stains behind.

"Oh and, son?"

"Yeah?"

"No making out up there, okay." Jake's eyes twinkled. "You're on the clock."

Dan shook his head. "On the clock?"

"Yep, Charlie and I will be waiting down here. Any sign of trouble and we'll come up."

"Thanks, Jake," replied Dan, knowing they weren't talking about catching possums or him and Alice making out. Staring one's past in the face required back up. "Appreciate that."

Dan walked across the grass to where Alice and Muttley stood sunning themselves now the mist had evaporated. Her smile quivered as he approached, her shoulders tensed. He held her gaze until they stood close then he took her hand in his.

"Ready?"

She nodded, her fingers gripping his like a vice.

"Yell out at any time if you want to stop."

"I can't go back now, Dan. It's been too long already."

Dan released her hand and tucked her in under his arm. "Let's go then."

Together they walked toward the pub. At the door, Alice paused. "Thanks."

Dan pressed a kiss to her temple. "Don't thank me yet. God knows how many of those buggers are up there or what they've done to the place." He pushed open the door and led her inside.

CHAPTER NINE

*A*lice waited for the slap of anxiety as she peered into the pub, but it never came. She took in the polished jarrah tables, the newly tiled floor and the absence of plastic chairs. The pub sported a new bar counter and shelves on the wall that would soon hold an array of bottled mixers. Posters between the tall windows sported vintage adverts and potted herbs lined the sills. It no longer resembled the place of her nightmares and broken dreams.

"It's changed so much." Slipping out from under his arm, she ran a hand across the timber top on the bar. "You've put a lot of love into this, City Boy."

"I guess I have. I'm glad you approve. Dodge made the timber top and he's making the new bar chairs to match. Feel like checking out the new kitchen?"

The first step towards letting go had been painless, could she hope the next would be just as easy? The kitchen was the last place she and Pete had stood, yelling at each other as their dreams crumbled. The place she'd pushed too hard. Pete, standing outside in the rain, angry at the world, car keys dangling from his hand. They'd closed up after yet another night of slow service when Pete had angrily tossed aside the tea towel.

Fuck this, I'm getting out here.

What do you mean? Where are you going, Pete?

Away, away from you, from this stupid town. I'm going west to the mines, where the money is. Where there is life beyond a dusty main street and a handful of shops that haven't grown in over forty years.

Why? Why do you hate this town so much? Why do you hate me?

I don't hate you, Alice. I just don't love you anymore. I tried to tell you that, before the wedding, before the baby. Your dreams are here, they always have been. My dreams are out there somewhere. I want to find them before it's too late.

We can work it out. All marriages have ups and downs. Please don't go.

But even as she'd said it, Alice had known it was too late. They'd outgrown each other, two young kids brought together in a small community who'd let themselves get carried along with the tide of expectations.

Is this the life you want, Alice? A run-down pub in Nowhere? Scraping together a living in a dying town? We could have a real life in the city.

I don't want to move to the city. I want to raise our child here where Charlie is, where we grew up together. I want that same life for Lochie.

Grow up, Alice. There is no fucking life left in this town.

You're wrong!

Well then tell me what else there is to do here in Fuckedville? What future do you see here for us, for our child?

She'd met his question with silence, unable to answer it. Young, naïve, she'd believed all they'd needed was each other and the life they were about to bring into the world. She was so tired of having this same argument, day after day—her trying to talk him out of it, him refusing to budge.

Exactly—none! I'm done here. I'm going, with or without you.

That's right, run away. Run away like you always

have when things don't go your way. You destroyed this pub, my father's dream, because you can't see past your hatred for this town.

Of course, all this is my fault! Getting you pregnant—I did that all by myself, didn't I? Even when I told you we weren't ready for kids.

Pete had yelled and she'd fought right back, all the way out the back door and into the rain until he got behind the wheel of the car. She'd gone after him, ripped open the passenger side door.

You can't keep running, Pete. Someday you'll have to grow up. You have a responsibility to me, to your child.

Angry beyond reason, Pete had gunned the engine, his focus on getting away.

You can't drive like this. Come inside, let's work it out. Please?

In or out, Alice? The choice is yours. Either way, I'm getting the hell away from here tonight.

She should never have got in the car that day, but in that moment she'd known she had to stop Pete from driving away, no matter what state their relationship was in. She'd loved him since they were toddlers. Maybe she'd thought that after driving for a while he'd calm down. Perhaps she'd believed she could talk him down, like she'd used to when they were teenagers and he'd railed against the restrictions of small town life. So she'd got in and clipped on her seatbelt, trusting him still to take care of her and their baby, believing they could work it out.

No sooner was her door shut than Pete had pressed his foot flat to the floor, sending mud flying through the car park. She'd clung to the dash, terrified when reality sank in and she realised Pete wasn't slowing down.

Pete, stop!

But it was too late, the road was slippery with residue oil, the bend in the road came fast and all she saw was the tree bearing down on them, felt the back-breaking impact and heard the scream of tearing metal before blackness took over.

Dan's hand came down on her shoulder, drawing her back to the present. "You okay with this, Al?"

She nodded. She had to be okay with it. Tentatively, she stepped around the bar and through the door to the kitchen. The space bore no resemblance to the grotty seventies cookout it had once been. Shiny new appliances gleamed under the lights Dan flicked on.

"Mum's going to do the cooking—simple pub meals and taster plates. She's looking forward to opening night. She's got Lou coming over to help. Tessa and Dodge are babysitting the twins."

Alice smiled, sniffing back the tears memories brought with them. "I can see her out here in her apron, swinging her rolling pin. She makes a damn good omelette."

Dan's arm slipped around her waist and she sank into his side. "We don't have to go any further if you don't want to. I can tell the CWA no to letting out the rooms."

She shook her head. "I'm okay. It wouldn't be fair on you, Dan. This is your business now. I can't let it suffer because I haven't been able to face the past."

He wiped a stray tear from her cheek. "We don't have to face it all in one day."

"Yes, we do." Turning into him, she stretched up and kissed his lips. "Thank you for putting so much love into the pub. It's all I ever dreamed it could be. Dad would be proud."

His arms tightened around her and he pulled her close. "I'm glad you like it."

Alice let her head rest against his heartbeat for a moment, drawing in its strength and his warmth. Whether she wanted it to or not, having Dan at her side was changing things—as if he'd lifted the veil on her life and she could dream again. But dreams were tricky things. There'd been a time when she and Pete were happy and their dreams all mapped out, until life intervened and reality had come crashing down. How much would happiness cost a second time around?

Pulling out of his arms, Alice swiped the moisture from her cheeks. "Let's go catch some possums."

"Are you sure?"

She nodded. "There should still be some hessian sacks under the stairs, if you haven't cleaned out in there."

"No." He grimaced. "I haven't touched the stairs."

"Well, let's go get them and get the show on the road." Alice squared her shoulders and stiffened her spine.

They gathered the sacks and took the first flight of stairs. On the landing, Alice stopped and breathed. Unlike downstairs where the sadness had been swept away with the cobwebs and the air smelled like orange oil and lavender polish, up here it smelled damp and forlorn.

She tried to shrug off the memory of the last night she'd been up there, happily pregnant, so sure that her and Pete's troubles would wash away with the rain, positive that as a young couple in love, they could fix anything together. How wrong she'd been.

Dan flicked the switch on the wall and a few of the upper hall lights flickered on. "All you have to do is say the word and we'll leave."

She pointed to the brown stain that spread out on the ceiling above them. "If we do, that will just get worse and your whole roof will come tumbling down the stairs. Not sure it will be a good look on your nice new bar. You can hold my hand if you're scared."

He slipped his hand into hers. "Scared of a few harmless marsupials? I'm more scared of Pamela Brown. Let's do this."

Alice took the remaining stairs a little slower. "Have you seen an angry possum?"

"No, and I'm not sure I want to."

"They're feisty little things and very fast. It's daylight, so they're sleeping now." Stopping at the top of the stairs, Alice drew an apple out of her pocket and dropped it into the hessian sack. "If there's a nest and it's empty, I'll have to relocate it."

"Jake built a possum house in the big tree outside."

"Good, because they can't be released too far from where they're relocated from or they won't survive." On her left, the doorway to Lochie's room loomed and Alice swallowed at the lump in her throat. She stumbled and felt the squeeze of Dan's fingers on hers. "I'm okay."

Could she make it past the doorway without looking in? If she did look in—

"Say the word, Alice."

"So the plan is to put the sack in the roof and lure the possums into it with the apple." One step forward. "When they wake up, they'll head for the smell and we'll be waiting, ready to tie it up and relocate them."

Another step, two more and she'd face her biggest loss—her child. She bit down on her lip, tasting the coppery tang of blood. Blackness clawed at the edge of her vision and pain gripped her throat like a vice as she got closer to the open doorway, but she pressed on.

"Alice?" Dan's voice whispered down the abandoned hall.

The weight in her chest threatened to crush her as she put her hand on the wall to steady her balance. "Depending on how many babies are in the nest—" She cursed the hitch in her breath. Maybe she wasn't ready for this. The need to turn around and run, to keep on running, gripped her body and she squeezed her eyes shut. The tremors began, crawling in slow and steady before gripping her muscles ruthlessly and shaking her until she thought she heard her teeth rattle together.

"It's okay, honey," Dan said, drawing her against him. "You don't have to do this." His arms came around her and he held on tight. "Tell me what to do and I'll set the traps."

Alice concentrated on the timbre of his voice, the soft words of reassurance, the feel of his breath against her ear—anything except the doorway she'd closed her eyes to. She'd come this far. If she turned around now, she'd never come back up here again. That wouldn't be fair to Dan, or the community of Bindarra Creek. What was the use of a pub with a floor of accommodation that couldn't be used? What if Dan wanted to move up there? He'd be looking for a place to stay soon. He couldn't possibly want to live in his mother's spare room forever. Could she bear the thought of him living amongst her memories?

Taking a deep breath, she pulled out of his arms and forced herself to take that last step inside the doorway. Tears stung her eyelids, blurring the room in front of her. There was Lochie's cot, waiting for the baby it would never receive. The once freshly laundered pile of baby clothes that would never be worn was still neatly stacked on the dresser. She remembered the kick in her womb when she'd talked to her baby in that room, promised him so much and then in a single act of anger and selfishness, killed him in a road crash.

She sank to her knees, rocking back and forth in the doorway, regretting the past, hating the future. That awful night after the crash, they'd placed him in her arms like a sleeping angel, let her hold him a while before taking him away to the morgue. The next few days had passed in blur of sedation and pain. She longed for that nothingness now.

Numbly, she felt Dan pull her back and sink down to floor with her in his arms. Back against the wall, he held her close to his chest as she cried.

Dan felt the sting of Alice's pain as her sobs tore at his heart. Over her head, the room looked peaceful as if the baby slept there and would wake at any moment. He wished he could take away her pain. He wished he didn't have to put her through this. What kind of a heartless monster was he bringing her up here? What kind of a town made a mother face her loss like this in the name of a stupid ball. Screw the

CWA and damn the Bushman's Ball to buggery for the selfishness of it!

He shifted Alice off his lap, stood then gathered her up in his arms. Slowly, he made his way down the stairs with her head buried in his neck and her tears staining the collar of his shirt.

Downstairs, a small group had gathered—Charlie, Jake, Maureen and Edwina Lette. Dan cursed the kangaroo that had wrecked his car, the circumstances that had sent him hurtling towards Bindarra Creek and the pain he'd caused Alice, not once but twice. Silently, Maureen held out the keys to her car and Dan took them.

"I'll come with ya," muttered Charlie, his words strangled.

Jake opened the passenger door of the car and Dan slid Alice onto the seat and secured her seatbelt. Charlie got in the back, keeping his hand on her shoulder. The silence in the car tore at his nerve ends as Dan drove them across the bridge to sanctuary.

Inside, Charlie led the way to Alice's bedroom. "I'll put the kettle on and get some tea into the girl."

"Sure, thanks." Dan put her down on the bed and drew up a throw rug from the foot end. Gently, he covered her shivering body.

Opening her eyes, she peered at him through wet, spiky lashes. "Please stay. Don't go."

How could he refuse when he'd gotten her into this state? Dan kicked off his shoes, lay down and gathered her in his arms. "I'm sorry, honey. I'm so, so sorry."

Alice buried herself against him. If she could crawl into his skin, he thought she might. He couldn't hold her tightly enough.

"You have to put the sack in the roof near the nest," she murmured against his throat.

"I don't give a fuck about the possums. They can stay up there."

"You'll hear them scurrying around when they wake up."

"I don't care."

"As soon as they're in the sack, grab it and twist the bag closed."

"Alice, forget the goddamn possums. Forget everything. We'll use upstairs for storage."

Her hands fisted on his shirt. "Take the nest to the tree and then set them free from the bag. They'll run up to check the nest."

Dan felt a sting behind his own eyes, but he let her talk because she needed to.

"Make sure you close the hole in the roof where they're getting in."

"Sure, I can do that."

"Thanks. And Dan?"

"Yeah?"

"Can you ask the ladies at the CWA to clear out those upstairs rooms?"

"Anything that makes you happy, honey."

"What is happiness, Dan? I don't know anymore. I thought I'd found peace at least. I was mistaken."

Dan had no answer for her as he stroked the mass of curls that hung damply around her face. It took ages, but eventually the tension left her body and Alice slept. Reluctantly, he eased his arm out from her and let her head fall gently to the pillow. For a moment, he watched her sleep. The flush of her cheeks against the pillows, the damp tear tracks from the corners of her eyes, his brave and beautiful Alice. In that moment, with his arms still full of the feel of her, Dan realised he'd fallen hard.

"She asleep?" Charlie popped his head around the door.

"Yeah."

"Come and have a cuppa before you go."

Dan nodded. In the kitchen, he wrapped his

hands around the mug of steaming, sweet tea. "Jesus, Charlie that went downhill fast."

The old man's eyes watered. "I know, son, but it had to happen. Sad as it is, she would never have faced those demons if you hadn't bought that pub. She'd still be wallowing in guilt and memories instead of living. They were young kids, not much older than Slim and Lanky. They'd grown up together, played together and it seemed like the perfect relationship when they hooked up." Charlie rubbed at his wrist, as if trying to erase an itch that wasn't there. "Pete wanted out of town and Alice wouldn't budge. She wouldn't survive a minute in the city, not even now. Then the baby happened. It was all too much for Pete. He was a good man at heart but his heart wasn't in Bindarra Creek. Even if the accident hadn't happened, those two would have split up eventually. Their dreams pulled them in different directions as they grew up."

"Will she be okay?" Dan couldn't imagine life in Bindarra Creek if he never saw her smile again.

"She'll be right, mate. It might take a day or two, but she'll be right. Our Alice is a tough nut."

The tea in the mug grew cold as the silence stretched in the kitchen. "I think I'm in love with her, Charlie."

The old man tapped his fingers on the kitchen countertop. "Then be patient and wait for her, young Daniel. She has her own way of sorting things through. When she's done that, she'll come looking for you."

In the darkened room down the hall, Alice listened to the murmur of Charlie and Dan's voices. She'd dozed off in the warmth and comfort of Dan's arms, but the moment he'd moved she'd felt the loss, the cold creep back in. When had she come to need him so much? With his arms around her, she was ready to step into the world again and without him the future would stretch empty and meaningless ahead of her—again. That only made her dependent on his presence, and Alice Pritchard was anything but dependent.

Oh, how the roles had reversed themselves. With Pete, she'd been the strong one, the motivator, the realist and seldom the dreamer. When he was gone, she became the breadwinner, the rescuer and Ranger Alice to whom everyone looked in a crisis. The role weighed more heavily now than ever before. Charlie was right. She'd existed for the last eight years, taking on more responsibility to mask the emptiness, to pass the time in her reclusive world of denial.

Would Pete have learned to love Lochie? Would he have finally settled in Bindarra Creek after spending a lifetime trying to leave? The memories crowded in like a dark veil, each one more painful than the last.

The pain of her past had stared her in the face today. The stale smell of the forgotten ruins of her dreams had forever replaced the scent of baby powder, love and laughter. The fear that she'd never see him again if he'd left that night, that everything they'd built together would be gone, that her baby would grow up not knowing his father. So she'd got in the car and had been left with neither. Lochie's first steps, his first words, his first day at school—all gone, all lost because of one mistake, one stupid, irresponsible, thoughtless decision made out of fear for the man she loved.

That was a pain she could never face again, no matter how much she loved Dan Molyneaux.

CHAPTER TEN

*T*wo days, twelve hours and twenty four minutes later with no sign of Alice, Dan bagged a family of possums and relocated them to the big bluegum outside. He had to keep busy or the need to go to her despite Charlie's advice—that she would come to him—would win out.

The beer garden was shaping up nicely, with the cracks in the concrete filled and the wooden frame of the patio repaired. The overgrown wisteria curling up the posts had been pruned back and shaped to grow across a protective layer of shade cloth to act as a rooftop cover. On the expanding wall mural, two adult possums and a baby danced a jig around a big bluegum.

Dan glanced at the screen on his mobile phone

and it reflected back at him in stony silence. No response to his texts or calls about the possums or the update that Muttley was now permanently out of his pouch. The joey had a fondness for porridge and crime scene television Dan wanted share with Alice. Where the fuck *was* Alice and how the hell was he meant to stay away when he knew how badly she was hurting?

An uncomfortable itch settled between his shoulder blades. Charlie hadn't been down to see Jake either since the day Alice had come to rescue the possums. Despite the old man's advice to stay away and let Alice work things out in her own time, he couldn't do that knowing something was up. He felt it in his gut. He called to the joey and headed for the bridge, taking the shortcut across the paddock to the sanctuary's enclosures.

He found Charlie tossing vegetable scraps into the chicken pen. "Hey, everything okay?"

The old man turned slowly. "It will be."

"How's Alice doing? I've been trying to ring her."

Charlie smiled sadly. "Alice has gone, son."

Dan's heart plummeted from his chest. "Gone? What do you mean *gone*? Where?"

"She's gone away for a while to sort things out,

gone hiking in Cunnawarra National Park, maybe a little further."

"She's gone hiking? Alone? *Jesus*, Charlie! People go missing and die out there alone. What if she falls and gets hurt? I'm going after her. Where's she heading?"

The old man chuckled. "Settle down, Romeo. The girl knows what she's doing. She wouldn't appreciate you storming in all over her campsite or God forbid, getting yourself lost out there and she'd have to go finding you. Best thing for both of you is that you focus on getting the pub open in time for the Bushman's Ball."

"Screw the Bushman's Ball. I'll see if Cam wants to host it on Bindarra Downs. Seeing Alice like that, it's not worth it."

"Son, you're thinking with your heart not your head. Having the ball at the Riverside will be like raising a tradition from the dust. In the short time you've been in town, you've tamed our hell-raisers, embraced our fundraisers and breathed new life into an old icon. It warms my heart to see my old boxing gym in use again. Jake and I get a kick out of watching you train the arrogance out of those two youngsters. We've needed something like that in town for a while now. I was just too damn old to do it."

"You're not too old to coach from the sidelines, you know." Dan grinned.

"I prefer being a spectator these days. Now go on, boy, round up those old biddies down at the CWA and get them cracking on clearing out upstairs. You've got an opening night to plan and Christmas is only days away."

"If you hear from Alice—"

"I'll tell her you stopped by."

"Thanks, Charlie."

The walk back to pub did little to take the edge off his unease. Ranger or not, knowing Alice was alone out there somewhere facing the perils of the bush didn't sit well with him. Deep down though, he knew Charlie was right. Going after her wouldn't solve a thing. She was too strong to need that.

Word must have got out, because as he and Muttley crossed the bridge all twelve-plus members of the CWA were gathered under the bluegum.

"Ladies," greeted Dan.

Edwina stepped forward to hug him. She held on a little longer and muttered a satisfied *hmm* when she let him go. Dan didn't try to stop the smile from spreading on his lips.

"She'll come back soon. Her healing is almost complete and she'll be free to love you."

Dan sighed. Sometimes Edwina's little insights cut too close to the bone, but he hoped to God she was right.

"I'm always right, young man. Now where do we start?"

This time he laughed out loud. "Upstairs. I've arranged some plastic tubs for all Lochie and Alice's stuff. The furniture can go into the shed under dust covers. Anything else, bag and tag for charity. Once the ceilings are fixed, we'll do a big clean up and paint."

With a chorus of agreement, the group set off inside the pub. Dan headed for the gym, stripped off his shirt and beat new life into the Jack Dempsey. He couldn't stand by and watch Alice's life being packed into boxes. Instead, when she came home it would be to a clean slate and maybe she could start a new life here—with him—in Bindarra Creek.

The trek on foot to the ranger's hut at the peak of Point Lookout at New England National Park tested the last of Alice's strength. The path went way beyond the visitors' walk. It might only be eighty-odd kilometres from Bindarra Creek but the seclusion would give her the space she needed to think. The steep incline reaching heavenward to a view she knew would bring peace to her heart. There was nothing quite like standing at the edge of the Great Escarpment at five thousand feet and looking over the beauty of the ancient Gondwana rainforest. Up here the air was clean and pure. The only sound that of the birds and the sway of the trees in the wind. Below her, the ranges unfolded across the landscape and meandered north to the coast. Today, with the clear skies above and the mist lifted, the distant sea blended with the sky like a shimmering mirage on the far north coast.

Alice closed her eyes and listened to the silence. What was Dan doing now? She pulled her phone from her pocket and snapped a few pictures of the scenery. With the limited signal up here, she could at least read his messages without the clutter of memories and regrets. There was a lot to be said for distance.

She could never have faced upstairs without him, but now that she had she was torn. Seeing Lochie's stuff—remembering, regretting. If only she hadn't gotten into the car that night, things could have been so different. If only she hadn't started the fight, or learned to let it go when he was in one of those moods, Pete and Lochie might be alive today. Hindsight was a bitter and twisted teacher.

Rubbing the chill from her arms, Alice turned from the view and entered the hut. The simple furnishings—a chair, a table and a camp bed—provided no warmth or comfort as they had in the past when she'd made her trips up here. Instead, the room felt cold and empty—soulless, lonely.

She lit the fire from the kindling set in the hearth, an unspoken agreement to never leave your fellow ranger without a fire. Her muscles cried out for a long, hot bath but she knew the best she'd get was a cold wash in the stainless steel tub.

Time to call in and let Charlie know she was safe. She hooked up the microphone and tuned in on an unused channel on the CB Radio.

"Break one-seven for Checkpoint Charlie, are you there, Charlie?"

"Ten-four, receiving you loud and clear. How are you, mate?"

Alice breathed a sigh of relief at the sound of Charlie's voice. Hearing it always soothed her nerves. "Ten-twenty at Point Lookout. The view is spectacular."

"Good to hear. I have a ten-forty-four from the publican. He says he misses you."

Her heart dipped in her chest and Alice couldn't stop the smile from stretching her lips. "Copy that."

"Any return message?"

"Tell him that's a ten-thirty-nine, message received, standby."

She heard Charlie's chuckle crackled over the airwaves. "The boy's a mess with worry."

"Copy that. Reassure him it's all A-okay."

"Copy. Don't stay away too long, Ranger."

"I won't. Night, Pop. Over."

"Night, Al. Over and out."

Alice turned the radio knob to standby and put the cast iron kettle to boil on the grid in the fire. She pulled her phone from her pocket and placed it on the table. Later, with a mug of freeze-dried coffee and powdered milk in her hands, she'd read Dan's messages.

Could she risk falling in love with him? When he'd held her close, she'd felt something for him she'd never felt with Pete. A different kind of love, a kind of affinity she'd only ever read about, like two parts that made a whole. But he was still a city boy. How long before Bindarra Creek became too small for him and he longed for the glitter of city lights? How long before the novelty of running an average-income pub wore off and the call of wealth lured him away? One thing she was sure of, Alice couldn't live through that again.

Stirring the water into her mug, she watched the granules dissolve. But when he'd held her, kissed her, soothed her, she couldn't get enough of him, the feel of his skin against her cheek, the touch of his hands on her hair, the hunger that burned in her belly at his kiss. Whether she liked it or not she was already head-over-heels, heading for heartbreak. If he were here now, she couldn't resist him, not even if she tried because Dan Molyneaux was exactly what she needed to rid her of her nightmares, to make a new start. All she needed to do was forgive herself.

Alice switched on her phone and tapped the icon for her messages, glad they'd downloaded in the sketchy signal.

3.30 pm Hey Alice. U ok?

3.32 pm I got those little bastards. Relocated to the bluegum, happy as pigs in possum poo.

3.40 pm Alice?

3.41 pm Curly says hi. Wants to know where the fuck u r.

3.42 pm You really need to teach that bird some manners.

4.03 pm Muttley's out of the pouch drinking beer.

Alice laughed out loud at that one. He knew that would normally get a rise out of her.

4.05 pm He's watching CSI. Is that a good thing?

"Probably not, Dan," she said aloud with a smile.

4.06 pm Wants 2 B a PI when he grows up.

6.30 pm Now I want to know where the fuck Alice is

Alice felt the sting of tears behind her eyes. Surely there couldn't be any tears left to cry? God bless him, he knew how to make a woman feel wanted. Now all *she* wanted was to hear his voice and feel his arms around her again. She cursed the isolation of the mountain for the first time eight long years.

00.05 am Night Alice, wherever u r. Stay safe and come home soon.

00.08 am I think I'm in love with you.

Her heart jumped in her chest and her hand shook on the phone.

00.09 am For your possum-catching skills.

The days dragged liked weeks and Dan cursed every minute that ticked by without news from Alice. Sure,

Charlie had said she'd been in contact and that she was okay, but that didn't stop a man from worrying, did it? Couldn't she do her thinking where he could still see her every day and know she was alive, if not one hundred percent okay?

The smell of fresh paint drifted down the stairs as Dan opened the front door of the pub. Today the new furniture would arrive and he'd have his hands full making beds in the five rooms upstairs and hanging fresh towels in the two bathrooms. Council had approved his licence application for accommodation on the upper level since the ceiling and wrap-around veranda were repaired.

The roof was fixed, possum-proofed and painted green to blend in with the rolling New England hills. Outside, Jake had hung Christmas lights along the upper level railing, ready to be lit up on Christmas Eve. All that was missing from his life was Alice. He wanted to share with her that moment the pub came to life, signalling a fresh start.

Out in the shed, Slim and Lanky had built a stage for the band to play on at the Bushman's Ball. The CWA had planned each decoration, each song and the menu within an inch of its life. The invites were sent out far and wide—families, couples, singles and plus ones. Dan looked both ways up and down the street but there was still no sign of Alice or her ute. Damn her.

"She'll be here, I feel it in my waters."

"Jesus, Ms Lette!" Dan held a fist to his pounding heart. "Can you send me a smoke signal or something next time?"

"Where's the fun in that?" She laughed the hoarse, crackling sound of a lifetime smoker.

"In your waters, huh? Are they more reliable than say—your cards or your crystal ball?" Dan gave her an affectionate hug, and then let go before she pinched his arse.

Edwina Lette leaned her old, wiry body against the warm wall of the pub. "You cheeky boy, but yes, generally my gut serves me best. See over there?"

Dan let his gaze follow her finger pointing east. "Yeah?"

"The highest mountain is Point Lookout. Keep your thoughts and your heart pointing in that direction. That's where Alice goes when she needs space. She'll be here in time."

"In time for what?"

Edwina Lette smiled. "In time for everything. I need a smoke. Got a match?"

"No, all open flame is banned until fire season is over."

"Goddamn it, how's a girl supposed to sneak one in around here with all this community policing?" she grizzled affectionately.

Dan looked down at her, amused. How had he lived without these people before coming to this crazy no-horse-but-do-have-a-donkey town? His time in the city seemed a lifetime away now and even his nightmares had decreased. Perhaps because these days his dreams were filled with Alice.

"And so they should be."

"You've got to stop doing that, Ms Lette. One day you're going to read a few thoughts you'd wished you hadn't."

Her eyes twinkled. "How do you know I haven't already?"

Dan grinned. "You're incorrigible. Here comes the truck. How's your skills at making neat sheet corners?"

"Got my own B&B to take care of, buster. Make your own beds." With a peck on his cheek, she turned to walk away. "Eyes and heart on that hill, boy."

Dan watched her go with a laugh, but his thoughts ran to the hills. *Come on, Alice.*

CHAPTER ELEVEN

The days ambled closer to Christmas Eve, to the night of the Bushman's Ball. Dan tried hard—and failed—not to worry about Alice. All he could get out of Charlie was that Alice was fine. If he heard it one more time, he'd go crazy.

"She's gone into Armidale to sort out a few things. She's fine, son."

"So you keep telling me," he grumbled. "Muttley's ready to be released into the wild. If he stays any longer he'll start supporting his own football team."

"Have they delivered your new bar chairs yet?"

"Don't change the subject."

Charlie laughed. "She'll be back in time to

release the mob at the sanctuary and she'll pack Muttley off at the same time. Only a while longer."

"How long is a while?" On the upside, Armidale at least had a reliable mobile phone signal. Maybe she'd answer his messages now.

"You all set for the ball?"

Dan shrugged. "All the approvals are in, so it should be easy from here on. I can't believe it's only a few days away." Had Alice only been gone ten days? God, it felt like longer. How long did it take for a woman to think? His thumbs typed out a message.

Tell me u r ok.

Charlie glanced over at him. "She won't answer you until she's good and ready."

Dan shrugged. When the phone pinged seconds later, he almost dropped it.

I'm ok. Tell Muttley stay off the beer. Carbs are bad for him.

He grinned. "I guess she's ready."

Come home and tell him yourself.

Charlie shook his head. "Love makes you crazy. I'm going to hang out with Jake, he's as normal as it gets around here. No sexting my granddaughter, all right?"

"Charlie! What do you know about sexting?"

The old man winked. "Before mobile phones we

had letters, you know. Used to shock the shit out of the postmistress in those days. No fun in *that* anymore thanks to technology."

Your pop says stop sexting me.

I prefer to do my sexting in person.

Dan read the reply, blushed and dropped the phone into his pocket.

Charlie laughed. "She is my granddaughter, you know. And if she's found her sense of humour," he nodded toward the phone now vibrating against Dan's hip, "She's on the mend." He walked away, chuckling under his breath.

Dan pressed the phone against his hip in the hope it would stop vibrating. Eyes on Charlie's retreating back, he pulled it out and pressed the button to read the message.

What, no comeback, City Boy?

When?

When what?

When will u sext me?

Soon, GQ, soon.

His finger hovered over the dial button. He needed to hear her voice. The phone buzzed in his hand.

Don't u dare ring me!

Why not?

Cos it'll get dirty.

How dirty?

V dirty. Did u mean what you said?

What did I say?

U luv me?

I said that?

Yep.

Delusional. That's what 2 much mountain air does 4 u.

Have proof.

Show me.

U betcha.

This time he did dial her number, but she didn't pick up.

Alice laughed as her phone rang and Dan's number flashed up under B for Bastard. The temptation to answer, to hear his voice was strong, but she had to be sure before she stepped out of her safety zone. She'd come to Armidale to talk to a counsellor about her anxiety, a step she hadn't been able to face since Pete and Lochie's death. Eight long and emotional days later, she'd progressed beyond the guilt and emptiness. Finally, she could move on. She could explore this growing attraction to the man who'd held her through the worst of it, and maybe just maybe, she could enjoy the feel of his arms around her and the touch of his hands on her skin.

Her finger hovered but she pulled her hand back and dropped the phone in her bag. No, when she spoke to him again it would be face to face, no holds barred. She missed his humour and silly comebacks. How would he feel when they had to let Muttley go? Chances were the roo would come back and not stray too far from the paddock behind the pub, but she couldn't tell Dan that in case it didn't.

Who'd have guessed the city boy would be raising roos and relocating possums? He was so much better at it than Pete was, even though Pete had grown up around the wildlife in Bindarra Creek. Pete, now she could think of him again with the youthful affection they'd once shared before adulthood had created an edge. She'd loved him with all her heart, but it wasn't enough to keep him. She accepted now it wasn't her fault, and even if the accident hadn't happened, they'd be apart today.

Fate had played a hand for a reason and even though Pete hadn't deserved to die so young, she had to accept it was meant to be and nothing she could have done differently would have changed his destiny. Her arms would forever be empty of Lochie but there was always a place in her heart for him and maybe, God willing, one day she'd have the strength to hold another baby in her arms and smell the sweetness of motherhood again.

As she headed into the hairdresser's salon, her phone beeped. She pulled it out of her bag and unlocked the screen.

We miss you.

A group selfie—Dan front and centre with Muttley, Charlie, Curly and Jake huddled around him. She tapped it and made it her cover photo.

You've got ur shirt on

Quick as a flash, he came back: *I can take it off for you.*

Her body tightened at the memory of Dan with his shirt off and the feel of his very nice arse under her hands.

No!

The next photo came through with the three of them with their shirts off.

Tell me u can resist this.

Alice laughed out loud, to the amusement of the occupants of the salon.

U grew real muscles.

Been working out. Wanna feel?

Oh God, yes. Her eyes roamed his body in the photo hungrily, but it was his cheeky grin that hooked her heart.

Maybe?

Come home, Ranger Alice. It's all yours.

GTG, city boy. Got a hot date.

A date???

Yep.

WTF? Alice?

She ignored the insistent beep as she gave the receptionist her name. When it didn't stop as she was seated in the salon chair, she turned the sound off with a grin.

"Your boyfriend?" asked the young girl as she tied the cloak around Alice's shoulders.

"A friend."

The girl's eyes flicked to the screen photo. "He's hot."

"I'll tell him you said so." She dropped the phone back into her bag.

CHAPTER TWELVE

*D*an cursed the silence from Alice, again. God damn it, who the bloody hell was she out on a date with? If it wasn't for the fact that he still didn't have a car, he'd damn well drive to Armidale and find her. Charlie chuckled behind him.

"It's not funny, Charlie. Who's she hanging out with?"

Charlie slipped his arms back into his shirt and slowly buttoned it up with arthritic fingers.

"How would I know, son?" His eyes twinkled.

"Do I need to be jealous?"

"You mean more than you are already?"

Dan sighed. "I just want her to come home and tell me she's okay."

"We all do." The old man tucked his shirt into his pants. "Come on, we've got work to do yet. Young Cam is off-loading the hay bales for the dance this arvo. Let's put those new muscles to the test."

Dan shrugged on his shirt, checked his phone—just in case—and followed Charlie up to the shed. He hoped the old man was right and that she'd be back soon. Not seeing her every day, not being able to judge for himself that she was okay was driving him crazy. He worked off his frustration like a madman, clearing the floor, separating junk from things he could use in the pub, then helping Cam off-load hay bales.

By nightfall, his back ached and there wasn't a muscle in his body that didn't hurt. He all but crawled into the office off the kitchen he'd converted into living quarters a week ago. A soak in a hot bath wouldn't go amiss but for now a shower would have to do. There was no way he was messing up the upstairs bathrooms after he'd cleaned them to a sparkle. The tiny cubicle off the office was a squeeze and would test the screaming power of his muscles, but at least it might ease the ache.

He stripped down, turned on the water and stepped in under the cold spray, swearing until it warmed up and sluiced down his skin. Scrubbing away the day's grime, his thoughts turned back to Alice. What was she doing? How was her hot date? When that thought made his stomach churn and his head hurt, he rinsed, turned off the taps and stepped out the cubicle.

Towelling off the damp, he walked across the room and pulled his phone out of the pocket of his jeans. No response to his texts, damn her. Tossing the towel aside, he flopped down on the makeshift camp bed.

How was ur date?

Okay, if she didn't answer, he'd turn the phone off and forget about Alice. It rang, making his heart pound. "Hey."

"Hey yourself, Hotshot."

"How you doing?" God, it was good to hear her voice. He closed his eyes and listened.

"Fine, really good, much better."

"Have a good time on your date?"

She chuckled and the sound hit him square in the groin. "It's killing you, isn't it?"

"You're killing me." He wriggled down on the camp bed and put an arm up to pillow his head.

"My hairdresser thinks you're hot."

"Great, does she want to go out on a date?"

"She's eighteen." Amusement lit her tone and Dan smiled a little.

"Tell her to call me when she grows up."

"I'm seeing someone."

Well fucking oath, cut me off at the knees and throw me to the sharks. "That's nice. Hence the hot date?" Dan struggled to keep his tone neutral.

"You're jealous?"

"I have no right to be. We're barely even friends." He sat up, groaned at the stab of pain in his back and reached for the gym bag he was living out of until the cupboards were put in.

She sighed in his ear, sending shivers down his spine and making him wish she was sighing for a different reason. Yes, damn it, he was jealous. With the phone between his shoulder and cheek, he pulled on a pair of trunks.

"I'm seeing a counsellor, Dan. It's helping."

Dan gripped the phone in one hand and ran the other through his hair. Relief swam through his veins and hope flickered in his belly. "That's great, honey. A big step in the right direction. So no hot date then?"

"No, no hot date."

"Can't say I'm unhappy about that." He paced the

floor of the tiny room. "Don't want you to rush into things, you know. At least, not until you've had a taste of city flesh," he teased. She laughed and he liked it a little too much. Alice could make his stomach dip and blood sizzle without even trying hard.

"So, what are you up to?"

"Lying around naked, waiting for you to come home." Satisfaction tingled in his blood at her sharp intake of breath.

"Totally naked?"

"Yep." Well, except for the jocks, but Alice didn't need to know that and he owed her payback for the hot date thing.

"Wow."

"You betcha." He stretched out the twinge in his back. Who knew hauling hay bales would be such damn hard work?

"Still living with your mother?"

"No, I've converted the office into living quarters. I can barely swing a cat in here. It's pretty cosy."

"Cosy's good." Her voice softened.

"No mattress, just a camp bed."

"Mattresses are overrated."

The breathy response had another of his muscle

groups stiffening up. "Are we talking dirty here, Alice?"

"Maybe, a little? I don't know. I just needed to hear your voice. I hadn't planned to call you."

"Talking dirty is like dating, you know that, right?"

"Is this our first date then?"

"Oh honey, it can be if you like." Dan ran a hand down his face and tried to still the surge of desire pumping through him. He'd have a helluva time getting to sleep tonight if they went through with this.

"I'd rather our first date be in person."

"Sounds good to me." He wasn't sure whether to laugh or cry as he contemplated the night ahead filled with counting sheep.

On the other end of the line, Alice yawned. "Tell me, what's happening out there."

"The place is looking good for the ball this weekend. The bar fit-out is finished, the kitchen is stocked and the beds are made upstairs." He heard the hitch in her breath. "It's all good, honey. The ghosts are gone. They didn't stand a chance against the Country Women's Army."

Alice's laugh shivered down the line and flowed

over him. "Don't you mean Country Women's *Association*? Does it look good, Dan?"

"With Pamela Brown in charge, it's an army, trust me." Dan settled down on the camp bed and described each room in detail for her. "I learned how to do hospital corners with military precision, thanks to the ladies. Want me to come over and make your bed?"

"I would if I was home."

"Mmmm." He stretched out and flexed his calf muscles. "Have to put a raincheck on that one."

"So, are you going to keep stalking me when I get home?"

He heard the exhaustion in her voice and wished he could kiss it away. "Is that what I'm doing?"

She laughed quietly, a slow and sexy sound in his ear. "Ten messages in the space of half an hour? I'd call that stalking."

"I'd call it determined, maybe even a little desperate."

"You don't strike me as the desperate type."

"I wasn't until I met you, now I'm all kinds of desperate."

"I'm going to sleep now."

And didn't that just put a whole new set of pictures in his head? Alice, warm and naked, cuddled against him, in his arms, doing sexy things together that had nothing to do with sleep. "Huh," he grunted.

"Yeah, I have a few things to wrap up tomorrow before I head back. Hey, Dan?"

"Yeah?"

"How are your nightmares?"

Dan thought hard and realised he hadn't had one for a long time. Maybe his ghosts were on the move too. "Better every day. Cameron Reid and I have become good mates. We share our war stories over a beer and a hay bale. It's helping." The war in Iraq had left its scars on Cam and the man's insight into dealing with the horrors of it was helping more than any counselling had.

"That's good, I'm glad. Sleep tight, Dan."

"Sweet dreams, Alice."

For a while after she'd hung up, Dan listened to the silence, not wanting to break the tentative connection they'd forged, until his phone automatically cut the call.

The rhythm of country music played by a live band poured out the shed on the heels of a warm glow from the lights. Alice pulled up the handbrake on the ute, gathered up the skirt of her new dress and hopped out. Closing the door, she took a moment to look around.

On the upper level the rooms were lit, casting a welcoming light across the newly painted veranda. Downstairs, the lights were on, but the action had moved to the shed. Alice had to admit the city boy had done well with his restorations. There was no sign of the unhappy, dilapidated shell the building had been for eight years.

On the left the beer garden, lit with colourful solar party lanterns, buzzed with activity. A spotlight shone on Slim and Lanky's half-finished wall mural where it nestled under the wisteria-covered patio. Alice smiled as the warmth of community spirit seeped back through her. As she made her way through the crowd, she was stopped, welcomed home and questioned with the kind-heartedness of people familiar with her struggle.

Finally, she could answer them honestly. "I'm okay, thanks."

Moving on up to the shed, she high-fived Slim and Lanky who were playing security at the door. Not that they needed security, the only gate-crashers they'd have here tonight might be a few creatures drawn by the light and smell of food.

"Hey fellas," she greeted. "Nice job on the artwork."

"Cheers," said Lanky. "Wait til you see what we add to it tomorrow."

The cheek in his grin had Alice shaking her head. She could only imagine what they'd come up with. In a relatively quiet corner to the side, Muttley lounged on a bed of hay, unperturbed by the noise around him. Alice rubbed his head and ears.

"Hey, little guy. Look how you've grown." Dan would be sorry to see the roo go, she knew, but that was how things worked in the wild.

"Alice, my girl, you're back." Charlie gathered her in for a hard hug.

"Hey, Pop. Miss me?"

"Always, my sweet. Everything okay now?"

She nodded. "Yes, all good. Looks like a big turnout tonight. I'm guessing the CWA are celebrating their success?"

"Not quite yet. Edwina is convinced there'll be more to celebrate before the night is out. It's been good though. All her rooms are booked out, Stevie's cottage up at the outdoor adventure place is hired out, the caravan park is full and so is Dan's paddock. Don't worry," he reassured her when her back stiffened and the ranger in her kicked in. "The CWA organised the fire permits and took care of the legal stuff while you were gone. They're keeping a close eye out for any trouble." He hooked an arm through hers and nodded toward the entrance to the shed. "Shall we?"

"Let's do it."

Arm in arm, they entered the bustle inside the shed. Immediately, Alice searched for Dan. There he was serving drinks behind the makeshift bar like he'd been born to it, the smile on his face full of humour as he joked with the locals. He looked every bit the part of a country boy comfortable with his surroundings and it made her heart pound at the sexiness of it.

The activity around her faded to white noise as she drank in the sight of him, his sun-kissed skin, the length of his hair where it now caressed his collar, the way his shirt stretched across his shoulders with every movement. God, she'd missed him.

At that moment, he looked up and saw her. His hand stilled mid-pour, the golden liquid in the glass and the skill of building a head on a beer on tap forgotten as he held her gaze.

Alice stood, her feet rooted to the floor as Charlie slipped away unnoticed. Nervously, her fingers played with the chiffon of her dress as she watched him finish pouring, hand the glass to Cameron Reid and wipe his hands on his bar apron.

Then he was walking toward her, tall and sexy in his black jeans and black T-shirt. It took all her strength not to run and meet him halfway. He stopped in front of her, toe to toe.

"Hello, Alice." His gaze burned into hers.

"Dan," was all she could manage as her breathing shallowed and her heart pounded. Her hands itched to touch him so she kept them anchored in the folds of her dress.

"I've never seen you in a dress before."

She let out a nervous laugh. "That's all you can say after two weeks of not seeing me?"

He stepped closer and pried her hands from her clothes, wrapping his fingers around hers. "I'd like to see you out of that dress."

Alice smiled. "That's so *not* original, City Boy."

His eyes twinkled with mischief as he disentangled their fingers, wrapped his arms around her and kissed her until the lights above them whirled in her vision. "Welcome home, Ranger Alice," he said when he let her come up for breath. "Would you take pity on a single bloke and be my plus one tonight?"

"Yes," she said, helping herself to one last kiss.

Slipping off the apron, he tied it around her waist. "Good, because I need help behind the bar. Come and look pretty next to me where I can keep an eye on you," he teased. "Don't want you running away again. Far too many single blokes around tonight. I don't want them getting any ideas."

"You're such a romantic," she grumbled.

He put his arm around her shoulders and drew her to his side. "Wait until we're alone, then I'll show you a thing or two about romance."

His eyes burned with promise and Alice didn't doubt for one moment he'd keep his word. So she spent the next agonising six hours alternately cursing and enjoying the fleeting touches of Dan's hands on her hips as he passed behind her, the brush of his body against hers in the tight space, the odd searing look when they had time to seek each other's attention, and the quick kisses he'd drop in random spots like her cheek or her forehead or the crown of her head, everywhere except where she wanted them—on her lips, on the rest of her body.

At midnight, Charlie decided he couldn't bear to watch it anymore. "Oh for God's sake, kids, go get a room. You'll be the death of me soon. My heart can't stand this anymore. Go! Jake and I'll finish here and clean up."

Neither Alice nor Dan argued. Instead, Dan yanked off their aprons, swept Alice into his arms and made short work of the distance between the shed and the kitchen door of the pub. In the kitchen, Maureen was cleaning up and polishing the stainless steel surfaces, ready for service the next day. As they passed her by, eyes only for each other, Maureen smiled happily and left, locking the kitchen door behind her.

At the door of his living quarters, Dan let Alice slide down his body and her feet touch the floor, but he held on tightly.

"Last chance to say no and slap me with a fine, Ranger."

"I've missed you too much to say no." She drew his head down to hers and kissed his lips with slow and loving reverence. "Besides, I've waited too long to get my hands on your arse. I'd rather slap that."

He grinned down at her. "My arse? That's all you want?"

"Hmm, I want to see if it's as feel-worthy as it looks. Then I'll check to make sure the rest of you comes up to speed."

Dan pushed open the door and walked her

backward into the room. The movement of his hips against her had her hanging onto him as the spiral of need turned her leg muscles to jelly. His body was warm and hard, and the barrier of clothing between them had to go so she could feel his skin on hers.

His hands moved to the zipper on her dress, lowering it to the rhythm of their breathing. It slipped off her shoulders with a whisper and he stepped back to let it fall between them. "You're beautiful, Alice. Please, don't ever leave me again."

Eyes on his, she reached for the belt on his jeans. "Give me a reason to stay."

"Gladly," he said, kicking the door closed behind them.

Dawn broke across the Riverside pub and Alice stretched contentedly on the camp bed. Dan Molyneaux did indeed have a very feel-worthy arse, stamina, and ways to make a girl feel very, very well loved. She couldn't get enough of his skin against hers, the feel of him around her and his extremely talented lips on her body. But it went even deeper than that, this love she felt for him in the pre-dawn hours of the morning. He made her feel whole again, like she could face anything as long as he was there beside her.

Slipping on the shirt he'd discarded the night before, she stepped out of the room in search of him. He stood at the front door of the pub, a mug of coffee in hand, wearing nothing but a pair of boxer briefs, and stared out across the still empty Main Street, deep in thought.

"Are you going to share that coffee?"

He opened his arms wide for her to step into. "Hey, beautiful." He pressed a kiss to her lips before hugging her to his chest.

"Hey yourself. What are you doing out here scaring the locals in your underwear?"

"Watching the world come alive, thanking the gods."

She grinned, pulled away a little and took his coffee mug, sipping the warm, sweet contents. "I thought you'd thanked them enough last night."

"Not nearly enough." His hand slipped down to stroke the base of her spine and draw her closer.

Alice let her hand wander across his body, enjoying the tightening of his muscles under her touch. "Dan? I think I'm in love with you."

He stilled under her hands, tipped her chin up so he could see her eyes. "You think?"

She nodded.

"Oh honey, that's the best news I've had since I bought the pub. But *think?* What will it take to convince you?"

"Come back to bed and we'll work it out."

Stepping out of his arms, she took his hand and led the way across the wooden floor towards his bedroom. Around them the rising sun filtered in through the windows, making the shadows slowly disappear.

"I might take some convincing," she warned.

"I like a challenge." Tugging on her hand, he gently pulled her back against his chest. His hand skimmed the skin on her stomach, drawing her hips back into the cradle of his. "I know all the sweet spots."

Alice breathed through a surge of desire as he touched one of those spots now, tilted her head back against his shoulder to receive the kiss he pressed to the pulse that raced in her neck. The touch of his skin against hers was a drug she never wanted to be free of. His clever hands found her breasts, favoured each of them before he turned her in his arms.

Tilting her face to his, he kissed her sweetly, tenderly, taking his time until she thought she'd go insane without tasting his tongue on hers.

"Love me, Dan," she whispered against his lips.

He lifted her up into his arms so her legs tangled around his waist, the essence of each other touching, teasing.

"I already do," he whispered back.

His hands caressed her bare bottom, drawing her into him, the barrier of his trunks a nuisance between them.

"I'm banning underwear," she muttered.

He hugged her closer, nipped at the skin on her shoulder, making her squirm against his hardness. "I'm fine with that."

He lay her down on the camp bed and for a moment simply looked. Everywhere his gaze touched, she burned. She tugged him closer by the elastic waistband of his trunks, took a moment to appreciate the way they caressed his form before she hooked them down and appreciated the raw view she'd come to prefer.

"You talk too much, Dan Molyneaux."

"You think?" He straddled her hips and lowered his mouth to hers. The time for small talk had passed.

Much later, with Dan's heart beating erratically under her ear and their skin slick, he murmured, "I'm not sure how much more of that action this camp bed can take. We might have to migrate to a mattress."

Alice smiled and kissed her way up his chest to his lips. "I have a perfectly good bed at home. Want to share it with me?"

"Are you suggesting we shack up? Alice! I'm shocked. What will Charlie say?"

She lifted her head to look at him. "I want to wake up with you every morning, fall asleep in your arms at night. I don't want to waste one moment without you, Dan."

His hands came up to cup her face. "I like the sound of that."

He kissed her sweetly and Alice drew every ounce of love from his lips he was willing to give. "Me too," she whispered.

"Alice?"

"Yes, Dan?"

"When you're ready, will you marry me so we can make babies together?"

Alice breathed through the shaft of pain at the mention of babies. Her mind wandered over the excruciatingly frank sessions she'd had with the counsellor in Armidale.

Could she? Could she bear to have another child, older and wiser as she was? They'd talked about it at length—her concerns about another pregnancy, the memories and fears it would raise, but most of all they'd talked about the ultimate reward—fulfilment.

Lochie would always be her firstborn and it was okay to love him forever, but the grief and pain had gone, cleaned out of her mind as surely as Dan had cleaned out upstairs. As a mother she could never forget the choice she'd made that horrible night, but she could forgive—herself, Pete and their circumstances—and remember the good times and the blessings, but the time for mourning them had passed.

Dan's arms tightened around her. "I'm happy to keep practicing until you're ready, whenever that might be. No pressure, honey, no pressure at all. It's something we must both want together because I'd like to raise my children here in Bindarra Creek with you. And if you can't bring yourself to have another baby, we'll just have to raise Muttley's instead. I don't care, as long as we're together."

She studied Dan's face, the promise in his eyes, felt the comfort of his arms and the hardening of his body beneath hers. One thing she couldn't imagine was life without Dan Molyneaux.

"Yes."

"Yes what?" he asked, running his talented

fingers up the length of her spine, making her arch her back and press her hips into his.

"Yes, I'll have your babies."

"Yes!" he shouted, then the room fell silent except for their whispers and the loving sounds of two lost souls finding each other and coming home.

The End

NOTE FROM THE AUTHOR

Thank you so much for taking the time to read my story *Home to Bindarra Creek* which is part of the Bindarra Creek Romance series.

If you would like to know more about upcoming releases or would love to talk anything book related, please join my street team at Book Love with Juanita Kees or sign up for my quarterly newsletter. I'd love your company.

All reviews are appreciated.

Look out for the brand new Bindarra Creek series, *A Town Reborn* from July 2019.

Keep reading for an excerpt from Promise Me Forever (Bindarra Creek – A Town Reborn) *by Juanita Kees*

PROMISE ME FOREVER

Bindarra Creek A Town Reborn

JUANITA KEES

Can Meg win Jack's heart, change his view of country life and prove to him that Bindarra Creek is a town worth fighting for? Find out February 14, 2020.

*J*ack Hughes hitched his backpack higher onto his shoulder, perched his sunglasses on his head, loosened another button on his shirt and contemplated all the things he'd done wrong in his life to deserve being sent to hell.

Bindarra Creek, somewhere between Armidale and Moree, a town reborn out of fire and flood and God only knew what else. A dot on the map of New South Wales where a few die-hards hung onto hope that new life could be breathed into the quiet streets.

A town where his producer had sent Jack to lick his wounds. Out of the spotlight, away from trolling Twitter feeds, heartless critics and fake news click bait.

And to make matters worse, he'd had to walk the last four kilometres because his beloved EH Holden, Betty, had carked it on the outskirts of town with steam pouring from under her bonnet. Now she was at the mercy of any passing road trains that would likely sweep her right off the side of the road.

As if poor Betty hadn't suffered enough after his ex-girlfriend had taken a knife to her right-hand side fender and left her scarred for life. An action sparked by a whole string of unfortunate events he didn't want to think about when his feet were on fire in his shoes.

Reaching the address his boss had given him, Jack waved off the flies and opened the gate outside Mary Moonie's Museum. Stepping onto the cracked concrete path, the tune from *Deliverance* played on a loop between his ears. The place was a verandah post short of falling in a heap. The old iron roof sagged, red paint making way for a coat of brown rust. Dust coated the glass of the wood-framed windows, the paint chipped and peeling. All it needed was a bloke on the verandah with a shotgun, and his producer's day would be made.

With a grimace and a prayer that the warped door wouldn't fall off its rusty hinges, Jack pushed it open. He blinked against the brightness of the fluorescent lighting inside what once might have been an impressive gift shop and entry display. Relics from the town's tumultuous history now looked worse for wear and bore a few obvious signs of water damage.

He welcomed the blast of cool air that touched his face. At least the air conditioning was fairly modern. He eyed the rumbling unit—probably fitted in the seventies—with dubious delight. The door squealed shut behind him. Dabbing at the sweat on his forehead with his bandanna, he approached the 1920s counter and the lady behind it.

Only about twenty-odd years younger than the shop counter, she looked ready for a day at the races. Black fringed dress dating back to the era of swing bands and jazz clubs, clip-on earrings he remembered seeing in old photos from the fifties and sixties, and a fascinator in her recently coloured, rusty-blonde hair. A multitude of mixed vintage bangles circled her left wrist while her right one sported a dainty marcasite watch. She would have been one classy lady back in her day.

"G'day," he said.

She smiled at him, tipping her reading glasses lower on her nose. "G'day, love. What can I help you with today? We have our self-guided tour on special at thirty dollars."

Self-guided tour of what? The crumbling dunny out the back? Jack flashed his press pass and returned her smile, his mouth dry and his lips a little sunburned. "Jack Hughes from Channel Eight, *Outback Affairs*." The words soured on his tongue. He used to be Jack Hughes, *International News*. His producer hadn't even lined up the film crew yet, not sure there was even a story worth covering out here in The Arse End of Nowhere. "Here to cover the story of Mary Moonie and Bindarra Creek, a town reborn."

He tried to keep cynicism from colouring his tone and failed. He'd done his research. Reluctantly. How many chances did a town get at rebirth before the residents gave up?

"That'll be forty-five dollars entry fee then." The smile froze on her lips and she pushed her glasses firmly onto the bridge of her nose.

"Forty—What? Are you serious?" All Jack wanted was a cold drink from the antique fridge, but now he was too scared to ask the price.

"Does this look like the kind of face that would crack a joke? This isn't just any old museum, you know. This is where Mary Moonie lived. And where she died. Right there in that corner." She pointed at the rocking chair in the corner of the shop, her black-painted and pointy nails almost claw-like on her crooked, arthritic fingers. "Her life has historical significance. Don't mess with me or I'll up it to sixty dollars." She rang up the threatened amount on a cash register straight out of an old western movie and held out her hand. "And for the record, I didn't want the press involved. Cash only, no credit."

"Aunty Phyllis!"

Jack turned towards the back of the shop and Hell suddenly got a lot more interesting as an angel dropped in. Or maybe he had heatstroke. A woman with white-blonde hair and almost translucent skin, wearing khaki shorts, a hot pink T-shirt, steel-capped boots and a breath-stealing smile emerged from the shadows at the rear of the shop.

"You must be Jack?"

Soft, silvery tones tickled his spine, fizzed his blood and tied his tongue in knots. He nodded as she approached. In the flicker of the fluorescent light above the counter, her skin glowed soft and pearly, like the satin of his sheets at home. Her eyes met his, neither green nor blue but some captivating colour in between. His breath hitched in his throat.

"This is my Aunty Phyllis and I'm Meg, Mary's granddaughter."

Jack couldn't help but stare at her exquisite features as he engulfed her delicate hand in his. A flash of fire spread in his belly at the sparkle in her eyes. Hooley dooley hotness. He remembered a story one of his teachers had told at school once about a fairy who lived in the outback and lured men into the bush with her beauty. For the first time since his childhood, Jack wondered if the legend was true, because the girl with her hand in his was truly something else.

His brain ramped back into gear as the raspy cackle of the extortionist behind the counter broke the spell that bound his tongue.

"Jack Hughes, *Outback Affairs*. I believe my producer contacted you?" Reluctantly, he let her hand go when she tugged at it, and the blood fizzed back into his head along with what was left of his common sense. Women were trouble and he couldn't let this one distract him from his job or he'd never get back to reality.

"Yes, we were expecting you to arrive hours ago. Come with me and I'll take you over to the Riverside Pub. That's where you'll be staying while you're in town." She shook a warning finger at the old dear behind the counter. "Aunty Phyl, stop trying to rip off the tourists. We want to encourage them to come inside, not chase them away," she said as she swept past Jack, opened the fridge, and took out a bottle of water.

"Got to get cash flowing into this mausoleum somehow, my girl."

"Not that way. And it's a museum, thank you very much. If Granny Mary heard you call it a mausoleum, she'd come back to haunt you." Meg handed Jack the bottle of water. "Here you go. It's hot out there today. I'm sure you'd kill for a beer instead."

Aunty Phyllis huffed out a breath. "I'd use those words lightly considering what happened to Mary."

"There's no proof she was poisoned." Meg shot a warning look across the counter then turned to Jack to explain, "Her heart gave out."

See, no story at all. Jack shifted on his feet thinking that, in this possibly crazy town, he'd still sniff whatever was handed to him anyway, just in case. Could you smell poison?

"Right." Aunty Phyllis drew the word out on a sceptical note. "You tell that to those fancy city laboratory people next time they're testing the drinking water. Someone is trying to kill the people in this town."

Meg shook her head. "The contamination could have happened after the flood. All kinds of chemicals and junk got washed into the river when it rose. Come along, Jack. The beer is bottled in Sydney and the drinking water has been given the all clear. As long as you don't go drinking still water from any billabongs out in the bush, you're okay. Besides, Dan who owns the Riverside Pub wouldn't kill a fly."

"Or a cockroach," muttered Phyllis with a pointed look at Jack as she reached for the fly spray beside her. "Gotta keep the pests under control, you know."

With a quick look at Aunty Phyllis, Jack dropped his sunnies over his eyes and followed Meg out the door onto the pavement. What the hell kind of town had his boss sent him to?

The view on the other hand was pretty damn pleasing. Meg had a sway to her hips that was easy to watch. A man could get used to that. If he was in the market. But with Kelsey leaving him over the stir Tamryn Hollister had caused with that fake video, he'd be avoiding women for a while.

Shit. How could he have forgotten all about Betty? Jack dragged his gaze from Meg's hips. "Wait

... My car. I had to leave it down the road. She overheated. Any chance we could get it towed in?" He stopped and waited for her to turn around.

"Oh dear. That could be a problem. Is it a rental?"

"No, she's all mine." He couldn't help the proud grin that split his face because even beat up, Betty was the love of his life. The only girl who hadn't given him any trouble. Until today.

"Oh dear."

He didn't like the tightening of her lips or the frown that brought her perfect eyebrows closer together. "What do you mean 'oh dear'?"

"Ever since Nobby Wilkie went bush after Mary died, some of the local kids have been collecting abandoned cars to build a spirit garden to bring him back. Nobby likes to tinker and he teaches the kids how to fix things."

A headache began a slow thump behind Jack's eyes. He pushed his sunglasses back up onto his head and rubbed the bridge of his nose. He couldn't let Betty die abandoned on the side of the road. She was all he had left.

Meg's warm, comforting touch on his arm had him dropping his hand from his face to look into those fairy eyes once more. Maybe she had a magic wand or something she could wave.

"Betty's a classic," he said, as if that would explain everything.

"Ahh…" She dragged the sound out on a sigh that sent pleasant shivers down his spine. "I get it. How about this? I'll drag *my* old ute out of the garage and we'll go and collect Betty. We'll have to work fast though, so that beer I promised you might have to wait."

"What do you mean 'work fast'?" He needed to get a handle on his words so he didn't keep repeating hers like a moron.

She stepped from foot to foot, squirming a little. "It's just … well … she could be mistaken for a wreck depending on the condition she's in and, if that's the case, you might find she's missing a few parts when we get there."

Jack cursed his boss, his ex, the bloody viral click bait video, and the town of Bindarra Creek as the vision of Betty—stripped bare—swam in his vision. God, he hated shitty backwater towns.

Bindarra Creek Romance series

A little about the Bindarra Creek Romance series:
13 months. 13 authors. 13 romances.

Welcome to Bindarra Creek, a struggling country town where people work hard and love deeply. Set in the picturesque tablelands of New England, Australia, Bindarra Creek is a fictional, drought stricken community full of intrigue, adventure, drama and romance.
Life and love in a small country town has never been more challenging.

Books in the Bindarra Creek Romance series:

Bindarra Creek Makeover - S. E. Gilchrist
Shadows of the Heart- Lee Christine
Second Chance Love - Susanne Bellamy
The CEO Mechanic - Sandie James
Reach for the Stars - Kerrie Paterson
Home to Bindarra Creek - Juanita Kees
Stolen Sanctuary - Stacey Nash
Tempting Fate - Erin Moira O'Hara

One More Day - Linda Charles
The Vine - Lauren McKellar
The Ghost of His Past - Simone Angela
Joanie's Dilemma - Marianne Theresa
Buckley's Chance - Noelle Clark

For more info on the other stories in this series, please visit:

http://bindarracreekromance.com/

ABOUT THE AUTHOR

Finding love and hope in small country towns with dark secrets ....

Juanita escapes the real world by reading and writing Australian Rural Romance novels with elements of suspense, Australian Fantasy Paranormal and Small Town USA stories. Her romance novels star spirited heroines who give the hero a run for his money before giving in. She creates emotionally engaging worlds steeped in romance, suspense, mystery and intrigue, set in dusty, rural outback Australia and on the NASCAR racetracks of America.

Her small town and Australian rural romances have made the Amazon bestseller and top 100 lists. Juanita writes mostly contemporary and Australian rural romantic suspense but also likes to dabble in the ponds of fantasy and paranormal with Greek gods brought to life in the 21st century. When she's not writing, Juanita is mother to three boys and has a passion for fast cars and country living.

Author Site: juanitakees.com

facebook.com/juanitakeesauthor

twitter.com/juanitakees

goodreads.com/juanitak

bookbub.com/authors/juanita-kees